MUSIC OF THE HEART

Susanna had given up her career as a concert pianist when her affair with the famous conductor Ralph Ewart-James ended dramatically. Now teaching in a quiet Norfolk village, she was convinced that her past was a secret. But her peace was shattered when a journalist recognised her. Against her will, Susanna found herself attracted to the journalist, but with the appearance of Ewart-James, Susanna finds herself thrown into confusion—would that old magic be rekindled?

Books by Jean M. Long
in the Linford Romance Library:

THE MAN WITH GRANITE EYES
CORNISH RHAPSODY
TO DREAM OF GOLD APPLES
ISLAND SERENADE
MUSIC OF THE HEART

JEAN M. LONG

MUSIC OF
THE HEART

Complete and Unabridged

LINFORD
Leicester

First published in Great Britain in 1984 by
Robert Hale Ltd.,
London

First Linford Edition
published July 1990
by arrangement with
Robert Hale Ltd.,
London

British Library CIP Data

Long, Jean M.
Music of the heart.—Large print ed.—
Linford romance library
I. Title
823'.914[F]

ISBN 0-7089-6882-1

Published by
F. A. Thorpe (Publishing) Ltd.
Anstey, Leicestershire
Set by Rowland Phototypesetting Ltd.
Bury St. Edmunds, Suffolk
Printed and bound in Great Britain by
T. J. Press (Padstow) Ltd., Padstow, Cornwall

1

THE concert ended amidst deafening applause. Blue eyes shining, Susanna turned to her father. "That was fantastic! Thanks for bringing me, Dad. You know how I adore Rachmaninov."

"Hmm—it was good, I'll admit, but you would have played it even better, Susie."

She smiled. "At one time, perhaps." Just for a moment she closed her eyes and recalled another concert hall where she had been the pianist and Ralph Ewart-James the conductor. Those days seemed to have a shadowy, dreamlike quality about them now.

As they reached the foyer her father touched her arm. "Isn't that your headmaster's wife over there—talking with that fellow in the grey suit?"

Cynthia Bryant spotted them almost

1

simultaneously and beckoned them over. She shook Robert Price's hand and then turned to Susanna.

"My dear, you look absolutely charming—such a pretty dress. Wasn't it a splendid performance?" Without waiting for a reply she raced on, "Do let me introduce you both to Mark Liston, our new English master. Graham was snowed under with work so Mark offered to accompany me tonight. Mark, this is Mr. Price and his daughter. They live in Bridgethorpe and Miss Price teaches piano at Ravenscourt College."

The slimly built man with a thatch of russet hair greeted them politely and then startled Susanna by asking:

"Haven't we met somewhere before, Miss Price?" Dark eyebrows arched questioningly and amber-flecked brown eyes met her midnight-blue ones. Susanna returned his gaze levelly, even though her heart beat had quickened.

"No, I'm afraid you must be mistaken," she told him coolly, but, even as she spoke, she had the uneasy feeling that he was right for there was something vaguely familiar about that soft cultured voice and those disturbingly expressive eyes.

Cynthia Bryant patted her beautifully coiffured hair. "You've probably seen Miss Price around the village, Mark."

"Yes, you're no doubt right. As I'm resident at Ravenscourt, I came early to get settled in before term began," he informed Susanna. "It's a beautiful setting for a boarding-school, isn't it?"

She nodded, practically convinced that she hadn't seen Mark Liston in Bridge-thorpe, and yet the feeling that they had indeed met before persisted. Fairly tall and immaculately dressed, she judged him to be in his mid-thirties.

"Did you enjoy the concert?" she asked him now, making an effort to be sociable. He gave her a captivating smile, making her aware of what an attractive man he was.

"Oh, yes, very much indeed." There was something far too serious about this young woman, he reflected. Her honey-blond hair was scraped back unbecomingly into a knot and the large, round spectacles gave her an almost owlish appearance. It was her hands he noted particularly, however—beautiful, soft and slender, ending in incredibly long fingers. Piano fingers, his mother would have said. A distant chord struck in his memory. Had he met her before on some other musical occasion—in another concert hall perhaps?

As they drove home along the narrow country lanes which riddled Norfolk, Robert Price said, "Had you seen that fellow Liston around before, Susie?"

"Not in the village and yet, well I don't know if it's my imagination playing tricks, but I certainly do have the feeling that we've met somewhere previously, although for the life of me I can't place him, and the name doesn't ring a bell . . . Oh, Dad, I do so hope he hasn't recognised me."

"You're afraid that he might be a voice from the past, eh?" her father asked

4

gently. "Well, would that really be so very terrible? It's bound to happen one day, darling. I'm proud of the fact that my daughter is Susanna Rosenfield, the once celebrated concert pianist, and have never understood why you want to conceal the fact."

"Oh, Dad," Susanna sighed, "I've told you often enough. I left that life behind me when I returned to England. It was my choice. All that is over now and I just want to forget it."

Robert Price's eyes clouded over. He had never come to terms with the fact that his daughter had abruptly thrown up a brilliant career midstream. The excuses had been made to the public that she was suffering from nervous exhaustion through working too hard and that she needed a long rest, but, unfortunately, the newspapers had told a very different story. Ralph Ewart-James, a man whom Robert Price despised without even meeting, had a lot to answer for. So far as Robert was concerned it was Ralph who was responsible for ruining

Susanna's happiness and for involving her in a scandal which had virtually finished her career overnight.

"Watch out, there's a rabbit!" Susanna cried suddenly, interrupting his thoughts as the headlights picked out the small creature. Her father swerved sharply.

"I don't think I hit it—would have felt a bump—they get mesmerised by the headlights, I suppose . . . Nearly home now, Susie—just as well with that long journey ahead of me tomorrow. Are you sure you won't mind being left alone in the cottage whilst I'm up north?"

"Of course not, besides, I shan't be alone. I've got Tabitha to keep me company."

Her father laughed. "That cat! Your Aunt Jessie sounded so desperate on the phone that I felt I simply must go to Yorkshire."

"Of course you must." She thought affectionately of her recently widowed aunt. Her uncle's affairs were in a muddle and the little village grocery stores was proving such a headache that her father had volunteered to go up to help his sister sort matters out.

During the two years that they had lived in Bridgethorpe, father and daughter had scarcely been separated. The isolated existence had suited Susanna and gradually the pain of her affair with Ralph had eased.

"It's a pity you haven't made any real friends in Bridgethorpe, Susie," Robert Price said now.

"Friends have a strange habit of evaporating when you most need them," she said bitterly. "Don't worry about me, Dad, I've got plenty to keep me occupied what with my piano teaching and the garden, and I can always go up to Yorkshire for a weekend if I feel in need of company. And, of course, just so soon as George Purbright goes into hospital for his hip operation I shall be taking over all his music lessons at Ravenscourt, as I've told you . . . And so, you see, I really shan't have time to get lonely."

"Perhaps I ought to leave you the car," her father said.

"No, your need is greater than mine. It's just a pity that Aunt Jessie sold the van in such a hurry."

Her father changed gear. "Yes, but I suppose she needed some ready cash. You're going to be pretty stuck without transport, Susie."

"I can always get a taxi if I'm really desperate so just stop worrying, Dad," she reassured him. "I shall be perfectly all right, you'll see."

"Goodbye, Miss Price. I'll look forward to seeing you on Monday."

Susanna stood at the cottage gate and waited until Graham Bryant's car had disappeared from view. It had been an eventful morning, she reflected. First she had waved her father off on his journey up north and then there had been a phone call from an urgent-sounding Graham Bryant who had told her that George Purbright had been offered a hospital bed earlier than expected and so could she possibly cope with all the extra music teaching right from the beginning of

8

term? When she had said that she could, just so long as he gave her until Monday to get herself organised, he had come over to discuss details with her there and then. To her amazement he had informed her that Mark Liston had offered to assist her with the class singing lessons.

Susanna was so busy with her piano tuition during the afternoon that she had little time to think about the new workload she had taken on at Ravenscourt College.

Annabel Davidson, the rector's nine-year-old daughter, was out of breath when she arrived for her lesson.

"It's all right, you're not late," Susanna told her. "Come along in."

Annabel set her music case down and struggled out of her anorak.

"Mummy had to go to the hairdresser's so I walked from the village," she informed Susanna, tossing back her dark plaits. "She told me to ask you to come to supper tomorrow night."

Susanna ushered her into the sitting-room. "That's kind of her, but I'm not sure if I can manage it. I'll have a word with your mother when she comes to collect you."

"She said she won't take no for an answer," Annabel told her firmly, seating herself gracefully at the piano. "Shall I do my scales first?"

"What? Oh, yes—go ahead." During the short time that she had been in Bridgethorpe, Judy Davidson had done her level best to take Susanna under her wing, trying hard to involve her in all manner of social activities, but she had found her task difficult because Susanna had doggedly refused to participate, usually using her father as an excuse to stay away from church functions. Now with her father in Yorkshire it seemed she was going to have difficulty in declining Judy's well-meaning invitations. Frantically she racked her brain for some other excuse.

After the lesson Judy Davidson hadn't turned up to collect Annabel and so Susanna sent the girl into the garden with a glass of lemonade whilst she made herself some tea. Eventually Judy arrived looking hot and bothered. Susanna waved aside her apologies.

"Not to worry," she assured her. "I always take a break now, anyway. Annabel's in the garden. Would you like some tea? I've just made some."

"Oh, that would be lovely—I'm parched." Judy attempted to tidy her recently cut fair hair. "I've just met Graham Bryant in the post office. He says you're going to take over from George Purbright."

Susanna collected another cup and saucer and placed it on the tea-tray.

"Yes, although I'm not too sure quite how much help I'll be because, what with all my own private piano lessons, I can only actually manage one extra full day and two mornings per week at Ravenscourt. Anyway, it's better than nothing, I suppose."

"Well, it's obviously taken a weight off Graham's mind at any rate."

Judy followed Susanna out into the garden. Annabel had discovered the tabby cat basking in the sunshine and was tickling its tummy. She waved to her mother.

"Do you do all this yourself," Judy enquired settling herself on the rustic bench and looking about her with interest.

"My father attends to the grass and the vegetable patch and I look after the flower borders. Of course, with him away I'll find it a bit tougher." She could have bitten her tongue the moment she had said it.

"Your father's away? Nothing's wrong, I hope?" Judy asked, her pleasant face full of concern. Susanna poured the tea and explained briefly.

"Well, Tom will come down with the Flymo if the grass gets beyond you, and if you feel like some company you know you're welcome to visit us—if you can stand the chaos—three children and two dogs can be a bit much at times. By the way, did Annabel mention tomorrow night? I was afraid I'd forget to give you my invitation."

"Yes, it's most kind of you, but . . ." Susanna trailed off as she realised that she had still not thought of a convincing reason to refuse.

"No buts—not with your father away —you really must come, I insist. It's high time we got to know one another properly. There are so few people of our age group in the village. January was a bad time for us to move in, but now we're just about settled—thank goodness."

Susanna knew that she must be a good eight years younger than Judy Davidson, but supposed she looked older than twenty-nine. They discussed Annabel's progress at the piano for a while and then the doorbell rang announcing the arrival of Susanna's next pupil. She got to her feet apologetically and Judy followed suit.

"We mustn't detain you any longer, Miss Price—the tea was much appreciated—come along, Annabel. I'll look forward to seeing you tomorrow night then at around seven thirty."

"Actually, I don't have any transport— my father's taken the car," Susanna said in a last desperate bid to back out of the invitation.

"That's no problem, Tom can pick you up after evensong," Judy told her, handing Annabel her music case. "Well, goodbye for now."

Susanna knew that she had used her father as an excuse for leading a quiet existence for far too long and that she could no longer hide behind him. Oh, why couldn't people just leave her alone? Mrs. Jenkins thought that her music teacher's silent mood was due to her own poor execution of the pieces and made even more mistakes than usual in her nervousness.

Over a solitary supper, Susanna reflected that Judy really was an extremely kind person to have so persistently bothered with her. The Davidsons had been living in Bridgethorpe for a mere three and a half months since the previous rector had retired. Tom Davidson taught RE and some Latin at Ravenscourt College, and so Susanna really knew him more than his wife. He was a very forthright, sincere person.

Judy had needed time to put the rambling Georgian rectory in order and now she was beginning to cast about for likely people to help her organise the various parish activities. Already the church was proving to be more lively than the parishioners of Bridgethorpe could remember it. Some of the older folk were not at all sure about the changes, but others welcomed them gladly.

During the evening Robert Price phoned to tell Susanna that he had arrived safely and that it seemed as if he might be in Yorkshire for quite some considerable time as things were in an even worse state than he'd anticipated.

After supper Susanna settled down to browse through the pile of music that Graham Bryant had brought along for her to see. Tabitha came to sit on her lap. Susanna shook her head over the archaic songs. George Purbright really was rather old-fashioned in his outlook. She wondered just how far she dared lean in the opposite direction without causing a revolution at Ravenscourt College. She contemplated attempting Herbert Chappell's *Daniel Jazz* for example. She wondered just what Mark Liston was proposing to offer in the way of help, and suddenly felt herself turning hot and cold. Surely he wasn't another ex-musician seeking refuge in Bridgethorpe? If only she could remember where they had met before.

As Susanna got ready to go to the rectory the following evening she wondered what on earth she would find to talk about. She had been undecided what to wear and had finally chosen a dress that her sister Catherine had bought her the previous Christmas. It had hung almost forgotten at the back of the wardrobe—a rather elegant creation made of some silky material in muted tones of smoky blue and silver grey in swirling patterns. Cathy had always had excellent taste.

Susanna had ceased to bother about clothes nowadays, telling herself that her profession made allowances for little eccentricities of dress. On tour she had always been rather Bohemian during the daytime, wearing loose Indian cotton caftans or jeans and sweat-shirts, and now she virtually lived in comfortable but rather drab skirts and jumpers, although she had plenty of evening wear.

She brushed her hair; it was the colour of rich golden honey and fell in waves some way below her shoulders—her crowning glory, Ralph had said. He wouldn't recognise her now, she reflected, twisting it into a classical style knot. The large spectacles completed the disguise for in those days she had worn contact lenses for most of the time. She applied a little make-up and realised that she had actually thought about her appearance for about the first time in over two years.

Tom Davidson arrived promptly at seven twenty and had the greatest difficulty in hiding his amazement when she saw the young woman who opened the door to him. She generally appeared rather dowdy, but tonight she actually looked extremely feminine. He was not to know that although she seemed poised and coolly elegant she was inwardly extremely nervous.

Judy appeared in the huge rectory hall to greet Susanna.

"Oh, this is nice—do let me take your coat and then there's someone I'd like you to meet."

Susanna swallowed hard; she had not realised that there was to be another guest. She followed Judy into the sitting-room and her eyes widened as she saw the man who was talking to Annabel, for it was Mark Liston.

"Mark, this is Miss Price who teaches piano at Ravenscourt College—Miss Price, Mark Liston the new English master who is also going to assist you with the music."

Mark Liston stretched out a hand in greeting; his deep brown eyes were filled with amusement. "Well, hallo again, Miss Price, I wondered when I'd run into you again—sooner than I'd expected."

"Do you two know each other?" Judy asked in surprise.

"Not exactly—I just happened to meet Miss Price and her father at that concert I attended with Cynthia Bryant the other evening."

"Oh—I see. Tom, fix Miss Price a drink will you, darling? I'm just going to check that nothing's burning in the kitchen."

Tom poured Susanna a Martini. "Where are the boys?" she asked Annabel who came to sit beside her on the sofa.

"Oh they're upstairs doing their prep. I'm glad I don't have to do any. They like the idea of having singing with you. I've been practising my new waltz tonight—would you like to hear it?"

"Not now, Annabel," her father interposed hastily. "We didn't invite Miss Price here to give you an extra piano lesson. On the other hand, if you would care to play something for us later on, Miss Price . . ."

"Oh, no, really," Susanna said hastily. The dogs wandered over to Susanna—one sniffed her shoes and the small terrier tried to jump on her lap.

"Get down—stupid dog," scolded Annabel, "or you'll spoil Miss Price's dress—I've never seen you wearing anything as pretty as that before," she said with the frankness of a child.

Mark Liston looked across and smiled. "She was wearing a pretty dress at the concert the other evening too—deep blue and quite long and sparkly."

Susanna coloured. It was a long time since she had found herself the centre of attention and she wasn't at all sure that she liked it. A warning signal flashed through her mind. It was evident that she was going or have to be on her guard even more than ever with Mark Liston around, if she wanted to keep her true identity a secret. She gazed round the untidy but comfortable room with its book-lined shelves and bright floral curtains and cushion covers and wondered what it must be like to lead Judy Davidson's kind of life.

Judy reappeared and picking up her

sherry-glass came to sit beside Susanna. "Well, this is nice—the time of the day I like best. I'm so glad you could come at last. My word though, it's taken an awful lot of persuading, but you see I was determined to persevere. Supper shouldn't be long now, providing there aren't any mishaps."

Tom turned to Susanna. "There's something I've been meaning to ask you for quite some time—tell me, were you christened 'Miss Price'?"

Judy laughed. "You'll have to forgive Tom for his direct approach, but he can't get used to the rather old-fashioned formality that exists in Bridgethorpe. He's told several of the parishioners to call him Tom, but they persist in addressing him as 'Rector' or 'Mr. Davidson' and it's apparently much the same up at the college, so do please call us Tom and Judy. Actually, I don't believe I know your Christian name."

"I do," Annabel piped up. "Your father calls you Susie, doesn't he?"

"Talk about little pitchers having big

21

ears," Tom said, amused. "What's it short for?"

"Susanna, actually, but it's rather a mouthful so hardly anyone ever uses it," she informed him, aware that Mark Liston was listening keenly.

Tom did a rapid calculation on his fingers. "Well, it's two letters shorter than Miss Price and much nicer."

"Good—that's the formalities dispensed with," Judy said. "Now, Annabel, the boys have just about finished their prep so upstairs with you and I'll be up to say goodnight presently."

"And Miss Price?" the child asked catching hold of Susanna's hand.

Susanna smilingly assented and Annabel obediently went upstairs.

"Come on Tom, you can uncork the wine for me," Judy said. "Mark, I'm sure you must have things to discuss with Susanna concerning your music teaching."

When they had gone out of the room Mark nodded towards the door and remarked, "She's a born organiser obviously. So what are your plans for the term's music then, Miss Price?"

Susanna was rather taken aback. "Well, I can only manage to take class music lessons on two mornings a week and an hour's choir practice during the evening after my private piano tuition is finished."

"Precisely—and I was engaged to teach English, not music, I'll remind you and so I had hoped for a bit of guidance."

Susanna was forced to smile. "Then I'm afraid it's going to be a bit like the blind leading the blind, that being the case. You see, I've never actually taught anything other than piano before—no class singing, nor percussion or recorder."

Mark regarded her in amazement. "Well, you're a cool customer, I must say. So how do you propose to set about it?"

Susanna outlined her ideas and he listened intently with undisguised admiration. "I have to take my hat off to you," he commented when she'd finished.

"You've certainly got it all worked out, haven't you?"

"Come along you two—supper's ready," Judy called from the doorway.

Over the delicious meal, Susanna felt herself gradually relaxing. She wasn't sure if it was the wine or the warmth of the room, but she realised that she was actually enjoying herself. She had to admit that she wasn't finding it nearly so difficult to socialise again as she had anticipated. It was rather as if she had suddenly been awakened from a long deep sleep. Judy was frankly amused and delighted at the obvious transformation in the rather prim music teacher, for she had been convinced that the young woman had hidden depths.

"Have you lived in the village all your life, Susanna?" she asked now.

"No, for just about two years now."

"So where were you before that?"

Susanna was conscious of Mark Liston surveying her with interest.

"We moved here from London," she

answered briefly, feeling herself clamming up. Fortunately, Tom came to her rescue.

"Judy has an insatiable curiosity about people—you'll get used to it—just ignore her if she gets too personal."

"Really, Tom," Judy protested laughingly. "Don't you find Bridgethorpe a bit quiet, though, Susanna? I mean you could bury yourself alive here and no-one would really notice."

"Yes, that's why I came here, because I like peace and quiet," Susanna told her and then immediately felt she had rebuffed her. Judy was ebullient however, remarks slid off her like water off a duck's back and she was soon gaily chatting on about her ideas to raise funds for repairing the church roof.

"More wine, Susanna?" Tom asked.

"Oh, no thank you—that was a lovely meal, Judy. Can I help you wash up?"

"Certainly not—Tom will help me whilst I'm making coffee and you can resume your discussion with Mark. Come along, darling."

Mark Liston examined the label on the

winebottle. "I figured that if you haven't taught more than one or two boys at a time you could have bitten off more than you had bargained for," he told her, "particularly if you're talking of doubling up forms for singing to fit it all in."

"Oh, I dare say I'll manage," Susanna told him, not feeling quite so confident as she sounded.

"Miss Price, have you any idea of the havoc thirty small boys let loose with percussion instruments might wreak?"

"Are you trying to scare me off?" she demanded, blue eyes flashing.

He sighed. "OK, I can see you're game for punishment, but don't say I didn't try to warn you. Look, how would it be if you took the lower forms single-handed and I came in to help with the doubled thirds, fourths and fifths?"

She considered this and then said, "Suits me—you sing then, do you?"

"Yes, I used to belong to an amateur operatic society a few years back, as a matter of fact."

They worked out a fairly satisfactory

arrangement, and Susanna suddenly felt a glow of pleasure at the thought of working with this man. Her father would be positively astounded at her sudden change of attitude. Judy popped her head round the door.

"Tom's just finishing the drying-up and then we'll have some coffee. I promised to say good-night to Annabel and she'll never sleep if I don't. Coming up, Susanna—or may I call you Susie?"

Susanna smiled. "Yes, of course you may. This is a beautiful old house, Judy."

"Yes, isn't it. Of course, there's a lot needs doing to it, and I'm a bit impatient." She led the way upstairs. "Now that your father's away, I was wondering if you'd like to join in with some of the church activities. I could do with some support and we could certainly use a pianist from time to time—particularly at our evening meetings."

"Judy, I'm sorry, but two evenings a week I'm teaching piano at home until eight o'clock, and there may be extra commitments at Ravenscourt," Susanna told her, feeling rather guilty.

Judy looked disappointed. "Yes, of course, it was selfish of me, I suppose, but there aren't many younger people about—apart from at the school. I confess I felt the need for someone to natter to."

The boys were asleep, but Annabel was wide awake and delighted to have a few moments' extra chat with Susanna. Afterwards, Judy took her into the spare room to show her a dress she was making, but it was obviously only a pretext.

"So, what do you think of him, then?" she demanded.

"Who?" Susanna looked puzzled.

"Why, Mark Liston, of course—don't you think he's charming?"

"He certainly seems very pleasant," she acknowledged. So that was why Judy had invited her to supper, was it? In an attempt to bring the pair of them together. Susanna supposed she must be one of the few prospective unattached females in Bridgethorpe. Well Judy had another think coming if she imagined that

Susanna was the slightest bit interested in Mark Liston other than as a colleague. She had finished with men for good.

As they reached the hall, Tom was putting down the phone. "I'm sorry, but I'm afraid I've got to go out—old Joe Dale's taken a turn for the worse. His daughter thinks it could be the end. I'm sure Mark will run Susanna home when she's ready."

When they finally left the rectory in Mark's Ford Capri he said:

"Nice family, aren't they? So welcoming. I think I'm going to like being here. Now you'll have to direct me. It's pretty isolated out here, aren't you bothered at being on your own?"

"No, why should I be? I've told you, I like peace and quiet."

He shot her a swift glance. "But have you always, I ask myself. Most people who bury themselves alive do so for a reason. I can't help thinking that."

"I could say exactly the same about you," she retorted. "At least I have my freedom—you've chosen to coop yourself up with one hundred and twenty small boys!"

He laughed. "Well, if I find it too much to bear perhaps I can call on the fair Miss Price from time to time. Who knows, I might even lure her from her cottage and entice her away to the city to attend another concert."

"I'm afraid you're wasting your time, Mr. Liston," she told him coldly. "You wouldn't find me at all good company. I'm not a very sociable sort of person."

He drew up outside the cottage. "I bet I could change all that—we'll just have to wait and see, won't we? OK then, I'll look forward to seeing you on Monday. Good-night, Miss Price."

A curtain twitched in a window of the adjacent cottage. It was practically unheard of for Miss Price to be out late twice in one week and with a gentleman too! Mrs. Gotobed was beside herself with curiosity.

Mark waited until Susanna had unlocked the front door before driving off. She was aware of a faint stirring inside her. There was something about this man that disturbed her, and the feeling that they had met before was stronger than ever. Surely fate could not be so cruel as to send someone from the past?

2

BEFORE it had been turned into a private school, Ravenscourt College had belonged to a baronet and still had an air of faded grandeur about it. Carefully tended lawns and flower-beds swept out beyond the terrace and, in the distance a line of Scots pines stood majestically against the skyline.

Graham Bryant always used the half-hour coffee-break on Monday morning as a time to make staff announcements. After explaining that Susanna was to take over from George Purbright with some assistance from Mark Liston, he then turned to the attractive girl seated beside him. "I am sure most of you have already met my niece, Amanda, who is here to assist in the office and to help my wife generally."

Amanda Bryant swept back her dark curls and smiled at all around her. The male members of staff immediately looked a little more lively and Susanna couldn't help wondering what Mark had to say about Amanda living in such an isolated place. Perhaps she was seeking a husband amongst the younger members of the staff. She surely couldn't be more than 23 or 24 and didn't look the type to be satisfied with leading a quiet life. It should prove interesting.

Graham Bryant came to sit beside Susanna. "Miss Price, I'd like to put you in the picture regarding one of Mr. Purbright's piano pupils. You probably encountered him at the end of term concert—Timothy Carstairs, a highly promising boy, I understand, although he doesn't always put his back into his other studies. His parents have recently become legally separated and the boy's taken it very badly. During the holidays the mother's gone of to the States with some film director . . . You may have heard of Julia Carstairs, the actress. The boy's father is in oil out in the Middle East somewhere and so he's been left in the

33

charge of his grandparents who live near Norwich. Timothy may prove resentful and difficult just now—particularly as George isn't here either—boy got on well with George."

Susanna listened sympathetically. "Yes, I remember Mr. Purbright mentioning him. Apparently, Timothy's already studying for his grade seven piano exams and he's barely 12."

Graham Bryant rubbed his chin. "Yes, well you may have to make a few allowances—thought I'd better fill you in on the background. Should you have any problems don't hesitate to come to me," and he drifted off to talk with another member of the staff.

Roger Marlowe, the young games master, came up to Susanna.

"I liked your rendering of *Onward Christian Soldiers* in assembly this morning, Miss Price. Old George used to make it sound like a funeral march. We all used to practically fall asleep, didn't we, Alec?"

Alec Kingsman nodded in agreement

and Susanna had to smile at the thought of anyone falling asleep during that particular hymn.

"I can see we're in for a lively term," Roger said with satisfaction. "What with you and Mark, and Amanda."

Mark Liston replacing his empty coffee-cup on the tray overheard and laughed. "We'll do our best not to disappoint you, Roger, won't we, Miss Price?"

"Gentlemen, may I remind you that the bell has gone," the deputy head said testily, and the staff scattered obediently.

Timothy Carstairs proved to be every bit as truculent and difficult as Graham Bryant had predicted. The boy surveyed Susanna sullenly and said mulishly, "I'm not awfully sure there's any point in my continuing with piano lessons this term with you—I may as well wait until Mr. Purbright returns."

"Oh, and why might that be?" queried Susanna trying to keep cool.

Timothy looked awkward and pushed back his rather unruly brown hair.

"It's just that Mr. Purbright and I are

used to one another, and I am pretty advanced—the furthest in the school, Mr. Purbright says, and so—well, I just thought that . . ." He trailed off.

Susanna thought she understood what the boy was attempting to convey to her. For some reason she had never questioned until now, she had always been saddled with beginners, those who showed little aptitude and certainly no pupil who had attained higher than a grade three standard. George Purbright, on the other hand, kept the cream for himself.

"I assume you evidently think that as I usually take the lower grades I won't have anything to contribute to your musical prowess," she enquired icily. He coloured slightly and Susanna said briskly, "All right, well let's give it a trial anyway. You never know, you might just change your mind. Now, sit down and play that rondo for me. Show me just what you can do, Timothy."

The boy, surprised at her cool air of authority and by the sudden use of his first name, an unheard-of thing with old Purbright, obediently did as he was told. Susanna intended to begin as she meant to carry on. He played the piece with expertise, but she was determined to make her presence felt.

"Oh, play it again," she commanded when he had finished, "and this time put some expression into it—you need to play from the soul, Timothy."

"Then show me how, Miss Price," he challenged her, greatly daring. She met his defiant and rather miserable grey eyes with her own blue ones and then changed places with him at the piano and played with all her being. As she ended the piece she found him staring at her with reluctant admiration.

"That was fantastic, Miss Price," he said and then added, "You played *Onward Christian Soldiers* pretty well too —shall I try again?"

Susanna had the distinct feeling that she had won him over, at least for the time being. He was exceptionally gifted, she recognised that, but rather inexperienced in technique and in great danger of becoming precocious. He was going to provide her with an interesting challenge.

Much to Susanna's relief the rest of the day went smoothly enough and after school Tom gave her a lift home. She felt unaccountably tired and sank thankfully into an armchair to read the newspaper for a few moments before getting her evening meal. As she flicked idly through the pages a familiar face suddenly sprang out at her from the gossip columns. She looked at the caption beside the photograph.

Well known conductor and composer Ralph Ewart-James relaxes at his Greek holiday villa with Christabel Vernon the talented young violinist who is to be seen frequently in his company nowadays . . .

The words spun before her eyes and she flung down the paper startling Tabitha. However hard she tried to put Ralph fro her mind there was always something to make her remember him. She had convinced herself that her affair with Ralph was over and yet, every time he was pictured with another girl, it still had the power to hurt. Would she never be free of him? Well there was one positive thing she could do and that was to cancel the newspapers until her father's return. Thus resolved she sat down at the piano and played furiously, her fingers flying over the keys.

"I adore this place. It's so gracious that it makes me feel a million dollars just to be sitting here," Judy enthused.

Susanna had jumped at the opportunity of a lift into Norwich, as she had some music to collect and now the two women were eating lunch in the Assembly House. Susanna looked about her; the restaurant with its chandeliers and elegant décor was one of the most delightful places to eat in that she had ever encountered.

"I think it's the atmosphere and, of course, in the early evenings you can find the theatre cast eating here. Years ago, apparently, this room was where the dancing took place."

Judy poured more coffee. "Yes, I can just imagine them dancing a minuet in here. So, what shall we do for the rest of the afternoon? Tom told me not to hurry back. He's seeing to the kids' tea and supervising prep etc."

"Well, actually I was thinking of popping into a couple of bookshops and then perhaps attending the choral evensong at the cathedral."

Judy looked a bit disappointed. "Oh, yes, that's a nice idea, but I had hoped you'd come and help me choose some material. I desperately need a new dress and it's so much cheaper to make it and then there's Annabel's summer frocks to think about."

"Well I'm sure we can fit it all in—I'd enjoy that," Susanna told her.

Judy sipped her coffee appreciatively. "This is a treat. I haven't been out for ages—so how's the first week gone, Susie?"

Susanna smiled. "I've enjoyed it, but I'm glad I don't work on Fridays or I wouldn't have time to breathe."

"And how are you making out with Mark Liston?"

"Oh, fine. He's very helpful." She had been pleasantly surprised to discover that Mark had more than average ability in both piano and singing and was grateful for his assistance.

"Of course he's been out of teaching for quite some time."

Susanna realised that Judy was itching to tell her something and forced herself to appear interested. "Really? What did he do previously then?"

"He was a journalist, apparently—a what-d'you-call-it. A sort of foreign correspondent. He's been all over the place."

Susanna's mouth went dry and she set down her coffee before she spilled it. Her worst suspicions had been confirmed. No wonder she had thought Mark Liston looked vaguely familiar. He had obviously been one of the many journalists who were always milling about during the concert tours. That explained why she had recognised his voice. He had probably shot questions at her like a report from a pistol.

"Susanna, are you OK? You're looking awfully pale," Judy asked her anxiously.

Susanna pulled herself together. "Yes, I'm fine, just a little tired, that's all. I'm sure I'll soon get used to my new routine." She picked up her handbag. "I think I'll just go and tidy up."

In the cloakroom as she applied fresh make-up she wondered why she had been such a fool as to suppose that reverting to her ordinary name and moving to a remote village would make her safe from the curious eyes of the world. What cruel chance had sent Mark Liston to Bridgethorpe? He held the trump card and when he learnt her identity it would surely only be a question of time before he revealed her whereabouts to the press. Oh, why couldn't she be left to live her life in peace and allowed to forget the past she was trying so hard to obliterate?

Surveying herself critically in the

mirror she consoled herself by the thought that it would probably be difficult for anyone to believe, looking at her now in her demure two-piece with the severe hairstyle and large glasses, that she had once captured the hearts of Europe and of Ralph Ewart-James.

Judy and Susanna spent a pleasurable time in the fabric shop.

"They're gorgeous, but I'm afraid I'm no needlewoman. I can't do more than sew a button on," Susanna said wistfully, as they admired the beautiful array of materials.

"I love sewing." Judy stooped to examine a price ticket. "Tell you what, if you see anything you fancy I'll make it up for you."

"Would you really? Well, I could certainly do with a new dress." Susanna pointed to an attractive rose-pink fabric. "How about that?"

"Oh, Susie, that would look lovely against your hair—hold it up. Yes, that's super. Now, tell me what you think of this for me?"

Judy had a knack of making Susanna become thoroughly involved in what she was doing and of drawing the younger girl out of her shell. Susanna realised that she hadn't enjoyed herself so much for ages.

The choral evensong in the ancient Norman cathedral was beautiful and restored peace to Susanna. As she sat listening to the glorious organ music all her problems suddenly seemed to fade into insignificance.

As they drove home that evening Judy said, "I have enjoyed today, Susie. We must do this again some time. If you like the dress I make you we'll come and get the material for another."

"You're very kind, Judy." Susanna suddenly felt extremely selfish for Judy was such a warm-hearted person. She had precious little time to spare and yet was prepared to help Susanna by dressmaking for her.

"I've been thinking," Susanna said on impulse, "if you really need me as an accompanist at your meetings from time to time, then I'll see what I can do."

Judy's face lit up. "Oh, Susie that would be appreciated. I really want Tom to make a success of this living. I can see you're going to be an asset to the community now that I've finally persuaded you to join in. There will be all sorts of occasions when we need a pianist and, although dear old Ellen Sillitoe does her best, she is inclined to make heavy weather of it."

Susanna smiled as she thought of the elderly lady concerned. "Well, I don't intend to hurt her feelings. Let her continue until she's had enough."

Judy slowed down to avoid a pheasant. "The livestock on this road is phenomenal. When the car was in dock the other week Tom had a lift with Sam Briggs and the old boy ran over a pheasant. Quick as lightning he shot out of the car and shoved it in the boot. Tom felt quite guilty."

Susanna laughed. "They have golden pheasants in Thetford Chase. It really is a beautiful spot. Dad and I often go there on Sunday afternoons."

"We haven't managed to get there yet, but we've promised to take the children for a picnic soon. Annabel's longing to see the deer. Have you always lived with your father, Susie?"

She had asked the question casually enough, but Susanna realised that the older woman was curious about her, and replied carefully:

"Oh, no, I had a flat in London at one time, but when my sister got married I came home again."

"And haven't you ever thought about marriage, Susanna?"

Susanna felt her throat constrict. "Oh, I'm quite happy the way I am. Life is what you make it, Judy. One has to accept what comes. Look, it won't be long now before the lilac hedges are out. They really are a picture along this stretch of road."

If Judy suspected that her companion was changing the subject she made no comment, and Susanna inwardly heaved a sigh of relief. When she arrived home there was a letter from her father telling her that it could be at least a couple of months before he had managed to sort things out in Yorkshire. Susanna realised that this could probably prove to be a blessing in disguise because being on her own had forced her to establish her own identity again. She realised that she was feeling more interested in life than she had done for many months.

Mark came into Susanna's music lesson to find a thoroughly engrossed second year enthusiastically crashing and banging percussion instruments in an attempt to capture the mood of some poems about the seashore.

"Different anyway," he said, and winked at Susanna. The end product was not at all bad and Susanna felt quite heartened. When the period was over Mark came to her side.

"I need to talk with you, Miss Price. When I was with the Head just now he mentioned the Speech Day concert. I thought you and I ought to have a discussion. Can you stay for school lunch?"

Susanna closed the piano lid. "I'm afraid not, Mr. Liston. I have a piano lesson at my cottage at two o'clock."

Mark's forehead creased in a frown. "So what time will you be free? We need to get this buttoned up pretty soon, you know."

"My lessons go on until eight o'clock tonight," she told him, collecting her music together. He did not look at all pleased.

"What about tomorrow?"

"I'm teaching here until five o'clock," she informed him.

At that juncture Amanda Bryant poked her head round the door.

"Sorry to interrupt," she said pertly, "but I'm going into Bury St. Edmunds with Aunt Cynthia, and wondered if you wanted anything, Mark?"

He smiled at her. "Can't think of anything off hand, Mandy—tell you what, though, Roger's desperately in need of some toothpaste. He's been using mine."

Amanda laughed and waved a list at him. "I've already asked him and just about everyone else. It's going to take me all afternoon to get through these errands. You won't forget we're playing badminton tonight, will you, Mark?" She gave him the sweetest smile and fluttered her ridiculously long lashes at him, and suddenly Susanna felt about 91 and very dowdy. She had the distinct impression that Mandy was deliberately letting her know about her date with Mark.

"Of course not—ciao, Mandy." She was gone with a wave of the hand.

"Do you play badminton?" Mark asked Susanna.

"No, I'm not the sporting kind," she replied rather curtly.

He shrugged. "A pity, you, Mandy, Roger and I could have made up a four-some some time. Now, I'd best go or I'll be late for lunch. We'll have to arrange a time to talk—I'll think round it."

As she went to collect her cycle,

Susanna found herself wishing that she could turn the clock back and be as extrovert and carefree as Amanda Bryant once again. Timothy Carstairs was waiting for her by the bicycle shed.

"Shouldn't you be at lunch?" she asked him.

"Yes, but I needed to see you." He didn't beat about the bush. "Just how good do you think my piano playing is, Miss Price?"

"Tim—can this possibly wait until tomorrow? I'm late as it is.

The boy shuffled his feet. "You see, I don't have any competition here, and I want to know how I'd compare with others of my age."

Susanna laughed. "You're asking the impossible. You are undeniably good, if that'll satisfy you, but a genius—well there aren't too many of those around. You'll make the grade, I can assure you, but you'll have to work hard. Fame doesn't just happen overnight you know. Now, I don't know what's prompted all this, but can we continue this discussion at a later date? Look, if you come to the music room tomorrow after lunch I can spare you a few minutes then—now run along or Matron will be after me."

The boy went deep in thought, hands in pockets like a careworn adult, Susanna suddenly thought pityingly.

Later that evening, when she was curled up in front of the fire with Tabitha on her lap, the phone rang. It was Mark Liston.

"Sorry to disturb you at this hour, but it probably won't be too easy to catch you tomorrow if you're stuck in that music room of yours all day."

"Who gave you my number?" she asked him coldly. "I'm ex-directory."

There was a pause and then he said: "Amanda Bryant found it for me in the office."

"Well that's a nerve! I only gave it to the Head for emergency use."

"Hey steady on," Mark told her, "I didn't think you'd mind—I thought the easiest way to discuss the concert would be over a meal so how about my taking you out to dinner tomorrow night? Say seven thirty for eight?"

Susanna was completely taken aback; her heart hammered wildly and she was just about to refuse when she remembered that it was only a business dinner with no strings attached.

"Well, thank you," she said weakly. "I trust it won't be anywhere too grand?"

He laughed. "You won't need to wear evening dress, if that's what you mean. I'll remind Amanda that you're ex-directory for future reference, if it bothers you that much. Good-night." And he replaced the receiver with an audible click.

Susanna was annoyed with herself for having made such a fuss. As she got herself a hot drink she realised that the thought of having dinner with Mark Liston was not altogether unpleasant. She would, however, need to be very much on her guard if she was to keep her true identity secret.

Timothy Carstairs bothered Susanna a lot.

She had the feeling that the boy was miserable, and, knowing the probable reason, could not delve too deeply. His playing was remarkable for a boy so young. She suddenly wished Ralph was in the vicinity so that she could ask his advice on the matter and was astonished that she had actually been able to think of her ex-fiancé in a detached manner for once.

"So why all those questions yesterday, Timothy?" she asked the boy when he came to see her in the small music room adjoining the library.

He perched on the edge of the piano stool. "I'd like to think I've got a future in music, but I don't want to be a second-rate musician—that's all. If I can't make it to the top then I'd rather not bother. I thought you'd be honest with me, Miss Price."

The boy was old beyond his years, she reflected, probably the result of too much adult company at home and too much time spent practising.

"It'll be years of hard work, Tim, if

you want to reach the top, but you mustn't neglect your academic studies."

"My grades were higher this week," he informed her, and then he added gravely, "My mother's having an affair with a film director and that would probably be an easy opening for me, wouldn't it? But I want to make it on my own merit."

From the window Susanna caught sight of Mark Liston and Amanda Bryant walking across the lawn deep in conversation. Mark had obviously said something amusing for Amanda suddenly laughed up at him. Susanna turned her attention back to Timothy.

"I've found a copy of the Chopin you wanted."

His face lit up. "Oh, great! Will you play it for me, please?"

"Well, I really think you ought to sight-read it, but all right, just this once."

Timothy listened intently and, as she finished playing she became aware that he wasn't her sole audience. Turning, she saw Mark Liston standing in the doorway.

"I'm sorry to interrupt, but the Head would like a word with Carstairs in his study now."

The boy looked startled and Susanna saw him tense up. "Thank you, Miss Price, that was super. May I go now?"

"Yes, of course." She waited until the boy had closed the door behind him before demanding frowningly of Mark, "What's he done?"

Mark crossed to her side. "Oh, nothing very drastic. He's been cutting games for extra piano practice and he needs the fresh air. Haven't you noticed how peaky he's looking? He seems rather emotionally disturbed at present."

"I'm not surprised with all that he's had to contend with at home just recently."

Mark nodded. "Yes, he's obviously taken it hard. You play superbly, Susanna. It must be soul-destroying having to listen to those kids mutilating music all day."

"Tim Carstairs is pretty exceptional, as a matter of fact," she said, colouring

55

slightly at Mark's sudden use of her Christian name. "He wants to be a concert pianist."

"Indeed—what an aspiration for a twelve-year-old!"

Susanna felt like retorting, "I wasn't any older when I made up my mind about a musical career." He rested a hand lightly on her shoulder and she felt as if he had branded her with a red-hot iron.

"Would you like to play that Chopin for me again?"

"I'd rather go and have a cup of coffee," she replied, suddenly desperate to escape from him, and he laughed. "Besides," she added, getting up from the piano stool, "Carstairs has got the music."

His brown eyes gleamed like polished mahogany. "I'm sure that's no problem. I'll bet you could play that nocturne from memory." And he was right, of course.

"You could have saved yourself the trouble of phoning me last night, after all," she said ignoring his last remark.

"It seemed to trouble you more than it

did me. You like your privacy, don't you, Miss Price?" He consulted his watch. "There're exactly fifteen minutes left before afternoon lessons, if you want that coffee . . . I'll pick you up at around seven thirty tonight then."

Arriving home at five thirty, Susanna waved to Mrs. Gotobed and wheeled her bike through to the shed. As she soaked in a hot bath and washed her hair she wished she could think of some excuse to avoid having dinner with Mark Liston. She felt very vulnerable where he was concerned, as if he knew all her past secrets—besides, she didn't know what to wear. In the end, she decided it would have to be the dress she had worn to Judy and Tom's the other evening.

"You want to be thankful, Tabby, that you've got such a beautiful coat," she told the cat as it rubbed itself round her legs. "You don't have to worry about what you're going to wear." Tabitha looked at her with large golden almond-shaped eyes and meowed.

By ten past seven Susanna was practically ready and was just deciding what to do with her hair when there was a loud crash from the direction of the kitchen. She raced downstairs to discover that Tabitha had climbed up onto the window-sill and dislodged a plant-pot which, in turn, had broken a glass vase on the way down.

"Oh, no!" Susanna gasped surveying the mess and, shooing the cat out of the way, hastily began to sweep up the debris. It wasn't until she felt a sharp prick on her finger that she realised she had caught it on a splinter of glass. The cut poured and she was still trying to staunch it under the cold water tap when the door-bell rang. She bound a handkerchief tightly round her finger and, rather irritably, went to open the front door.

"You're early," she greeted Mark. "I'm afraid I'm not quite ready because the cat's upset a plant-pot and I'm in the middle of cleaning it up."

"Not to worry." He stepped inside. "What have you done to your finger?"

"Oh, it's nothing—just a slight cut." She pushed open the sitting-room door. "Would you mind waiting in here whilst I finish tidying up?" Instead, he followed her into the kitchen.

"You'd better let me attend to that wound before you get blood all over your dress. Where's your first-aid kit?"

Obediently she fetched it and he carefully removed the handkerchief and gently bathed the cut. "Hmm, nasty." His contact with her wrist sent a curious tingling sensation down her arm.

"Don't put too much dressing on or I shan't be able to play the piano," she protested.

"You want it to heal, don't you?" he demanded. "There, that should do the trick." Much to her embarrassment he then proceeded to sweep up the rest of the debris.

"Would you care for a sherry?" she asked when he had finished.

"That sounds like a good idea." He waved the ill-fated cactus from the pot at her. "This poor thing will need repotting."

"I'll see to it in the morning—thanks." She led the way into the attractive sitting-room and he looked appreciatively at the chintz-covered suite and oak furniture off-set by pastel-tinted walls.

"This is a pleasant room and what a lovely piano!"

"There wasn't room for a grand, but this is strung like one."

She poured his sherry and handed it to him.

"I have to do something with my hair," she said rather self-consciously.

He surveyed her, head on one side. Her honey-gold hair was tied back with a piece of blue wool and swung silkily over one shoulder.

"Why? It's lovely like that and, what's more, it makes you look at least ten years younger." He suddenly reached out and touched it.

"Pure silk—it's a shame to hide it away —and now I know for sure who you remind me of. I suppose you weren't in Vienna about three years ago?"

Susanna swallowed nervously. "What an idea! As you can see, I lead a very quiet life here. Of course, they do say that everyone has a double."

He sipped his sherry. "Yes, I thought it would be too much of a coincidence, but it's a small world. Strange thing is, though, that the person I'm thinking of is also called Susanna."

"Really?" Susanna's heart was pounding wildly. "Well, if you'll just excuse me for a few moments, Mr. Liston."

"Oh, Mark, please. Of course, this girl I met didn't wear glasses and she wasn't nearly so serious as you. She laughed a lot. She was a pianist too—quite famous at that time—as a matter of fact."

Susanna, in a desperate bid to stop the conversation, said:

"I suppose you're talking about Susanna Rosenfield, although personally, I can't see any resemblance at all—apart from us both having the same colouring."

He stared at her uncertainly for a brief moment and she realised that she had successfully managed to call his bluff. "She disappeared, didn't she?" Susanna continued, before he had a chance to say anything. "I suppose the publicity was all too much for her—thanks for your help. I shan't keep you waiting long," and she hurriedly escaped upstairs.

In defiance of Mark Liston she pinned her hair into its customary knot. Her heart was racing, for she now knew where they had met before—at a memorable party in Vienna. No wonder she hadn't recognised him, for at that time he had had a beard. She recalled the occasion quite vividly now, even though she had forgotten about it until this very moment. She had been particularly exuberant that evening because the concert had gone so splendidly, and so she had been extra charming to the throngs of reporters and some of them had been invited to the party amongst them—Mark Liston.

She reapplied her lipstick and collected her coat. When she arrived downstairs

Mark was reading a music magazine with Tabitha sitting on his knee. The cat purred loudly as Mark fondled its ear.

"Tabby, I'm not at all pleased with you after all the chaos you've caused—get down," Susanna scolded.

Mark laughed. "She's quite a character, isn't she? Right, are you ready? I see you haven't taken my advice over your hair style, but never mind. Where shall we go? I confess I don't know this area too well."

"There's a rather nice inn which has a reputation for good food just over the Suffolk border—if that's not too far."

"Time's our own, isn't it? OK, you can direct me."

He spent the journey discussing the concert with her, so that by the time they reached their destination they had practically finished sorting everything out, rendering dinner quite unnecessary in her opinion. She then panicked as she wondered what on earth they would find to talk about for the next two or three hours.

The meal in the charming half-timbered inn was superb and after an initial period of shop talk they concluded the conversation and Mark said: "Right, that's enough of that—now tell me more about yourself. All anyone is prepared to tell me about you is that you've lived in Bridgethorpe for a couple of years, and that leaves a lot of background to fill in on, I rather think."

"One could say exactly the same about you," she rejoined. "You've turned up at Ravenscourt out of the blue, and Judy says you didn't used to teach, but were involved in journalism."

His face was expressionless. "Oh, so she told you that, did she? Right then, for every one fact that you tell me about yourself I'll give you one in exchange."

"Can't we just discuss music or something? My past isn't at all interesting." She willed him to change the subject.

He poured more wine and asked for the sweet-trolley. "I get the distinct impression that you've put up an impenetrable barrier and that you have no intention of letting anyone get to know you, Susanna Price, but I'm not to be fobbed off that easily. Yes, I was a journalist. I have an English degree and a teaching qualification, but after a short spell in a rather tough secondary school in London, I went to work in Fleet Street and gradually progressed until I got my own column on a well known daily. Now it's your turn."

Susanna sipped her wine and tried to appear calm. "I—I trained at the Royal College of Music . . ."

"Go on," he prompted her, his brown eyes curious.

"Mark, I came here tonight to discuss the programme for the concert, not to talk about myself," she said desperately.

"OK, if that's how you want it, but I'm warning you, I shall continue to persevere. I sense an air of mystery about you."

"That's ridiculous," she retorted rather too quickly.

"If you say so—now what will you have for dessert?"

She selected a slice of Black Forest

gateau. Realising that she had been rather abrupt she said: "It was kind of you to ask me out. I've enjoyed the meal. I'm afraid I've been a bit of a failure in the past—that's why I'd sooner put it behind me, if you don't mind. There was a time when I thought, like Tim Carstairs, that I could make it to the top, but it's not that easy and . . ."

"No, there wouldn't be any point if it were," he interrupted. "Do you have any other family besides your father, or is that subject taboo as well?"

She felt her colour rising. "No, of course not. I've a married sister in London, but we're very different types, and then there's my aunt in Yorkshire whom my father is staying with at the present moment and one or two cousins dotted about the globe."

"I take it your mother died some time ago?"

She concentrated on her dessert. "When I was in my early twenties. This gateau is superb. Do you have any family, Mark?"

"Yes, my parents live in Southwold, as a matter of fact, and I've a brother in Australia."

It was her turn to ask a direct question. "So why did you decide to give up journalism?"

He set down his pastry fork. "Pass. Oh, OK, I don't mind answering, really. I enjoyed many aspects of it, particularly the time I spent in Europe, but during these past months, I've been doing a stint as a war correspondent. Do you watch the foreign news?"

She nodded. "Then you've got your answer. It nearly broke me, Susanna, I don't mind admitting it. There were occasions when I was right out there in the thick of it, and one horrific time when I got bunged into prison. Yes, I could have applied to return to a more cushy number in London, but enough is enough. I suddenly wanted a change of occupation; a chance to recharge my batteries. Can you understand that, Susanna?"

"Yes, of course." He insisted on

ordering liqueur coffees and they went through into the cheerful lounge where a log fire blazed welcomingly.

"It's easy to let the world go by in a little backwater like Bridgethorpe," mused Mark. "Life just ticks on and nothing really happens. It's the perfect place to escape to when one's had enough of the big outside world, eh, Susanna?"

She smiled, "Yes, I like it in Norfolk and I'm happy enough with a quiet existence."

"So what are *you* hiding from, Susanna?" He said it so quietly that, for a moment, she wondered if his remark had just been a continuation of her own thoughts, but from the way those piercing brown eyes were surveying her, she knew that it had not.

"I'm afraid I don't know what you're talking about," she said.

He stirred his coffee. "I thought perhaps we were two of a kind, both seeking a refuge in Bridgethorpe after an unfortunate experience, but evidently I'm wrong."

She was unable to meet his eyes and busied herself adjusting the strap of her watch. "You do have some strange notions about me, Mark. Do you try to ferret out a story from every girl you take to dinner?"

He laughed at that. "You'd better put it down to my over-fertile imagination. To me you appear as Rapunzel locked in her tower."

Susanna was forced to smile. "Now you really are being absurd," she said lightly, but she was uncomfortably aware, however, that Mark might be watching for her reaction to his remarks in order to catch her out, and wondered just how much longer she could keep her secret safe from him.

"More coffee?" he asked her now. She declined and he drew her attention to the row of toby jugs suspended from the ceiling, pointing out the various different characters. She relaxed again.

It had been a strange sort of evening, she reflected as they drove back to Bridgethorpe a short while later. In spite of her misgivings she had enjoyed Mark's company more than she had thought possible.

"Thank you for the dinner, Mark. It's been a most enjoyable evening," she said as they approached the cottage.

"My pleasure—we must repeat it sometime." He caught her hand between his and she again experienced the same curious sensation, as if she had received a minor electric shock. "If you really want to show your appreciation you can play that Chopin for me again sometime. Well, I hope Tabitha hasn't upset any more pot plants."

"So do I—good-night, Mark." He sat in the car waiting whilst she walked up the path, and she noticed Mrs. Gotobed's net curtain was twitching and smiled to herself. She felt quite light-hearted as she prepared for bed. It was as if a veil had been lifted and she had awakened from a long deep sleep. Mark Liston was helping her to return to normality.

3

SUSANNA was cycling along the lane leading to Bridgethorpe church when Tom suddenly appeared, surplice flapping, from the direction of the rectory.

"Just the very person I wanted to see. You could just save my life, Susie. I've got my fortnightly Bible study meeting tonight and old Ellen Sillitoe's caught a filthy cold and so we're without a pianist. I wonder—could you possibly come along and play a few choruses for us? They do so enjoy a singsong."

Susanna readily agreed, realising that this would be one way of repaying the Davidsons' kindnesses.

"Thanks, Susie, you're a pal. I'll pick you up at around 7.45 p.m."

When Susanna arrived at the vicarage that evening she was greeted warmly by Judy, and ushered into the sitting-room

71

where she found a rather motley group assembled, including Mrs. Gotobed who looked astonished to see her next-door neighbour at any place other than the cottage.

Susanna enjoyed the meeting, in spite of herself, and afterwards, as they sat drinking coffee, found it a pleasant change from her own company. The dogs came bounding into the room, released from the kitchen, and greeted her rapturously.

"I expect they can smell Tabitha," she said to Mrs. Gotobed, as one of them pushed a wet nose into her hand.

"That cat of yours," rejoined her neighbour pointedly. "She's been sitting in my flower-bed again—quite flattened the lavender."

Susanna made sympathetic noises and agreed that Tabitha did indeed have a will of her own and then, catching Judy's amused glance, had the desire to giggle and bit her lip. Mrs. Gotobed's next comment, however, did not amuse Susanna.

"Your young man is a master up at the school, isn't he?"

Susanna was aware that all eyes, including Judy's and Tom's, were now focused on her. "I—I don't know who you mean, Mrs. Gotobed. Perhaps you've seen someone giving me a lift. I don't have the car with my father being away, you know."

"I mean that young man who took you out the other night—the one with the Ford Capri like my son's."

"That's Mark Liston's, isn't it, Susie?" Judy asked curiously.

"Yes," Susanna said shortly. She didn't intend to elaborate, after all it was none of their business and they could choose to think what they liked. Fortunately Mrs. Gotobed had come with her daughter-in-law, and so they left together.

"Can you stay on for a little while, Susie?" asked Judy. "I wanted to show you some patterns for your dress. I've just about finished running up Annabel's school frocks."

"Well, just for a bit then—thanks, Judy."

Tom closed the front door after the last of his parishioners.

"You mustn't mind them, you know, Susanna. They're dreadful gossips, but they don't see much life round here and so nothing goes unnoticed. I'm glad you're getting on so well with Mark. He's a nice fellow."

"Tom!" Judy said warningly.

Susanna smiled. "Oh, it's all right, Judy. It was only a business dinner. Mark wanted to discuss the end-of-term concert, as a matter of fact."

The idea of Mark Liston being her "young man" was proving an oddly disturbing thought, but she had absolutely no intention of ever becoming involved with any man again. Once she had had her fingers burnt, and she had resolved not to let it happen again.

When they had cleared away the coffee things, Judy showed Susanna the dress patterns and she quickly chose one tha she liked. Shortly afterwards Tom drove her home.

The previous day she had located her father's press-cutting album at the back of a cupboard, but she hadn't had an opportunity to look at it. She fetched it now. Tabitha woke up, stretched and came over to her mistress, purring loudly.

Susanna flipped over the pages until she found the cutting she wanted—an account of that glittering concert in Vienna which had been such a marvellous success. There was a photograph too—yellowing now—of her and Ralph Ewart-James. She read the review, and shut the book with a snap. How strange to think that Mark Liston had been present at that concert. The memory of that particular evening would remain with her for the rest of her life, for it had been the highlight of her career.

She realised that she had actually managed to look at a picture of Ralph without feeling upset. People said that time was the great healer; perhaps she was truly over her affair at last. She knew that she wouldn't have minded quite so much if only he hadn't asked her to marry him. They had even planned their honeymoon at his villa in Greece, where he had recently been photographed with the leader of his orchestra, Christabel Vernon.

"I know one thing, Tabby, you would have had to have watched your p's and q's if I had married Ralph," Susanna told the cat, stroking its sleek coat. "He doesn't care for cats." Tabitha blinked sleepily.

Later, as Susanna brushed her hair, she gazed into the mirror trying to see a reflection of her former self. She knew that the last two and a half years had matured her and that she had lost some of her giddy effervescence for ever but, below the surface, she was still the same. She might have a few scars, but they had only served to strengthen her character. She set down her brush with a sigh. Apart from the obvious physical attraction, there were times when she wondered just why she had loved Ralph so deeply. She felt herself grow hot as she thought about the way in which he had deceived her, allowing her to believe that he was free to marry even to the point of their becoming engaged. When she had finally learnt the truth, her humiliation had been so great that her immediate reaction had been to get as far away from Ralph and the orchestra as possible.

Susanna opened her dressing-table drawer and took out an ornate ring box. There, lying on a bed of velvet, was an exquisite emerald and diamond engagement ring in an antique silver setting. She knew it was worth a small fortune and supposed she ought to have returned it, but it served as a continual reminder of her reasons for being in Bridgethorpe—of the mistake that she must never make again.

"Ralph Ewart-James, you have a lot to answer for," she murmured. "The whole course of my life has been changed because of you. My future was neatly mapped out and then, overnight, it dramatically changed."

Beyond Ravenscourt College was a narrow country lane surrounded by cultivated fields and the occasional farm building. Susanna had been for a brisk walk before going home. She loved the Norfolk countryside, although some people found it bleak and desolate with its haunting skylines. The wind had loosened her hair and plastered strands across her face. She turned down a footpath that led to the school and, as she reached a small pine copse, Mark Liston suddenly appeared.

"Goodness, Mark, you did give me a fright!" she exclaimed startled.

Mark fell into step beside her. "I've been watching you for quite some time. This is an isolated spot and it's rather foolish of you to be walking alone. You might meet up with some unsavoury character whose intentions are not so honourable as mine."

Susanna laughed. "Are you trying to

scare me? I often come this way. I like to see the pheasant chicks at this time of year."

"Yes, there do seem to be rather a number round here. Mandy even spotted some in the school grounds the other day —a pity they're destined to satisfy someone's idea of sport."

"I take it you don't approve of shooting then?"

He shrugged. "I can't say I'm that keen. You look absolutely delightful, positively glowing and very untidy."

She felt the colour suffuse her cheeks. "It's this wind, and it's not very polite of you to make personal remarks like that." She attempted to tidy her hair.

"I meant it in the nicest way possible, as a matter of fact. I'd offer to run you home, but the Bryants have asked me to supper and so I'd better not risk being late."

"No, that's all right—I've got my bike." She finally succeeded in capturing the stray ends of hair and pinned them back.

"By the way, before I forget, your young reprobate Carstairs has been an absolute nuisance during the past week. He's managed to cross both Alec and myself on several occasions. The prep he's handed in has been disgraceful, and so I'm afraid we've had no alternative but to dock him his practising time until he's redone his work."

Susanna stared at Mark uncomprehendingly. "But you can't do that, he only gets an hour a day as it is and he needs every minute of it!"

"Then he ought to have thought about that beforehand. I'm sorry, but it's the only way he's going to learn that we mean business. I quite thought you'd support us."

"Well, I don't. The boy lives for his music—goodness knows he's got little else going for him and if you take that away what's left? I forbid you to do it—it simply isn't fair on him."

Mark frowned. "My dear Miss Price, we are going to beg to differ on this point. Carstairs has simply got to learn that he cannot be treated differently from anyone else. I will not make an exceptional case of him."

"Why not? He is exceptional—certainly the best pupil I've ever had. No, Mr. Liston you've overstepped the mark there. I shall have a word with Mr. Bryant."

Mark laughed shortly. "Don't worry, I've already done that and he's given his full permission. Carstairs is to have no more practising time until he redoes his Maths and English to our satisfaction."

Susanna gasped. "I can't believe it! Mr. Bryant knows what a bad patch Tim is going through."

"But being lenient is not going to help at this stage, I can assure you. He needs to feel secure and to do that he must have discipline."

"Well I think you're callous," she threw at him and marched furiously away down the drive to the cycle shed.

"Susanna!" he called after her, but she ignored him.

It wasn't until she was halfway home

that she began to cool down and she realised that it was a long time since she had become so heated about anything. She was aware that her storm with Mark had probably spoilt their relationship and, asking herself if that mattered to her, realised that it did.

Poor Tim, what would he do? She would have to see the boy, have a chat with him, but she wouldn't be at Ravenscourt College again until Monday.

On Saturday morning Susanna encountered Roger Marlowe in the post-office-cum-newsagents. He waved a women's magazine at her.

"Hi—I'm collecting this for Mrs. Bryant, just in case you think I've taken to reading the agony columns!"

She had to laugh, he was such a clown. He waited whilst she made her purchases.

"A group of us are off to Weeting to see Grimes Graves . . . You know, the Stone Age flint mines," He added seeing her puzzled expression. "And then afterwards we're having lunch in Thetford—fancy coming?"

Susanna smilingly shook her head. "Sorry, Roger, I'd like to, but I've already got a casserole cooking in the oven and I've rather a number of household chores to get through."

"A pity—but you are coming to the barn dance tonight, aren't you?"

"I wasn't even aware that there was one," she told him truthfully.

He sighed comically. "Don't you read the posters? They're everywhere. Look, there's even one in the window here! Well I shall expect to see you there and I shall claim a dance."

They left the shop and walked back along the street together.

"The others are waiting round the corner," Roger told her. "The girls were too lazy to get out of the car so I got the task of going to the shop—typical!"

Mark Liston was seated at the wheel of his Ford Capri with Amanda Bryant beside him, chattering animatedly. A pretty, elegantly dressed girl was sitting in the back.

Roger opened the car door and dropped the magazine onto Amanda's lap. "Look who I found in the post office."

Much to Susanna's relief, Mark's greeting was friendly enough. Amanda smiled and said: "Oh hallo, Susanna, this is my cousin Sally. She's staying for the weekend. Roger, you've been an absolute age. The others have gone on ahead."

Roger scrambled into the car beside Sally. "There was a queue—I asked Susanna to come with us, but she's in the middle of doing her housework."

"All work and no play . . ." murmured Mark, and she avoided his eyes.

"Are you coming to the barn dance tonight?" Amanda asked her.

"I hadn't really thought about it," Susanna hedged.

"Should be fun." Amanda put the magazine in her shopping basket. "Of course, it's not everyone's scene, I suppose. Aunt Cynthia says she wouldn't go if I paid her—too much noise. Perhaps you feel the same way?"

"Susanna is hardly in your aunt's age bracket," Mark commented. "I expect, being musical, she dances very well." He switched on the ignition. "Well, if you'll excuse us, Susanna, we'd better get a move on or we'll never get to Weeting this morning. Perhaps we'll see you this evening then?"

She muttered something non-committal and the others waved and shouted good-byes. She suddenly felt miserably out of it as she walked back to the cottage, although she recognised that it was almost entirely her own fault. Beside Mandy and Sally she felt dowdy and almost middle-aged, even though she was not quite thirty. To them she must appear an old maid. Once she, too, had been young and carefree, but nowadays she was probably considered to be a crashing bore. She mentally finished the proverb Mark had begun, "All work and no play makes Jack a dull boy and Jill a dull girl." It certainly applied to her.

As she walked along the lane in the direction of Lavender cottage she wondered if Mark had decided to forget their dispute or if he hadn't wanted to mention it in front of the others. She realised she would be relieved when she knew how things stood between them.

Mrs. Gotobed was leaning on her garden gate chatting to a friend. She waved to Susanna. "I was just telling Mrs. Baldwin here how much we enjoyed the singsong the other evening. Will you be coming again, Miss Price?"

"Probably," Susanna told her as she unlatched her own gate.

Mrs. Gotobed regarded her curiously. "You're looking a bit peaky, dear—missing your dad, I dare say. I've just asked Mrs. Baldwin in for a cup of coffee—how about joining us?"

"That's very kind of you," Susanna said on impulse. "I'll just take my shopping indoors first."

Mrs. Gotobed was justifiably surprised for, up to now, she had not succeeded in getting her neighbour to do more than pass the time of day with her. "Good, I'll go and put the kettle on then, dear."

As Susanna walked up her garden path she heard Mrs. Gotobed telling her friend, "She's such a quiet young lady and she plays that piano real lovely—got a beautiful touch—a pity she keeps herself to herself so much."

Well perhaps it was high time she became more sociable, Susanna told herself as she unlocked the back door.

Susanna spent the afternoon gardening. She was determined not to let things slide just because her father was away. When he had phoned the previous evening he had told her that affairs were moving very slowly in Yorkshire. Aunt Jessie was finding it very hard to adjust after her husband's death and Robert Price felt he could not leave his sister in her present state. Susanna had assured her father that she was coping perfectly well in his absence.

She had just filled a trug with weeds and was about to empty it into the wheelbarrow when she heard someone rapping on the front door. Opening the side gate she found Timothy Carstairs standing there.

"They told me in the shop where you lived—I simply had to see you, Miss Price," he blurted out.

Susanna felt she ought to take a firm line. "Aren't you breaking bounds?" she asked rather sternly.

"Not exactly—we're allowed into the village in threes on Saturday afternoons." He coloured as he saw her expression and mumbled. "We're not supposed to separate or come this far, but the others won't split."

"Well, you'd better come through."

The boy obeyed and stood awkwardly on the patio looking down at his shoes. Susanna removed her gardening gloves.

"As a matter of fact, Tim, I'm fully aware that you've been banned from practising, if that's what's the problem, and I'm sorry, but you've only got yourself to blame." She saw his face and realised that he had expected her to be more sympathetic, but it would have been totally unprofessional of her to make him aware of her true feelings on the subject. He looked so miserable that she softened.

"Look, I was just about to make some tea—gardening's thirsty work. Why don't you go and sit over there on the bench? I shan't be long and then we can have a talk."

She supposed she ought to phone Graham Bryant, but it surely wouldn't do any harm for the boy to stay with her until she had had a chance to talk with him.

Taking out the tea, a few moments later, she sat down beside him on the garden bench. He looked at her rather shyly and she realised that it was probably because of her appearance. She was dressed in jeans and a checked shirt and her hair, tied at the nape of her neck with a scrap of velvet ribbon, fell in a tangle of thick waves below her shoulders.

"I'm afraid you've caught me on the hop, Tim," she said, as one might to an adult. "I wasn't expecting visitors so I don't exactly look my best. Now, let's have it straight. Just why have you been letting me down?"

He looked at her shamefaced, obviously not expecting this. "It's all so unfair," he burst out. "Everyone's against me, but I thought you'd be different—I thought you'd understand."

"I'm trying to, Timothy, believe you me, but when I hear how you've behaved —it's not too easy." She handed him his tea.

"I had this letter from my mother . . ." he began.

Susanna pushed back a stray strand of hair. "Yes, go on," she prompted gently.

"She's in America with that film director fellow I told you about." He sipped his tea and Susanna waited for him to continue. "Well, she says she's not returning to my father—that she's going to get a divorce. How does anyone expect me to do my work properly with a thing like that hanging over my head? All I want to do is to be left alone to play the piano and they won't let me." The boy was on the verge of tears, and Susanna suddenly felt inadequate to cope with the situation. Tabitha sprang onto his knee and he stroked her absently.

"Look, Tim, perhaps things won't really be so bad as they seem now. I mean you'd probably see just as much of your parents as you do at present. It's always difficult to understand why people behave as they do, particularly when you care a lot about them." As she spoke she was thinking of Ralph.

Timothy's grey eyes were bleak. "I s'pose so, but it'll probably mean I'll have to spend even more time with my grandparents."

"Well, you don't know that so there's not much point in speculating, is there?" Susanna said briskly. She had a sudden inspiration. "Right now I could do with some help with the garden, so if you felt like making yourself useful I could ring through to Mr. Bryant to ask if you could remain here for a bit and then you could stay on to tea. I'll see that you don't get into trouble for breaking bounds."

The boy brightened. "I could mow the lawn for you," he offered and then he asked tentatively, "I suppose you wouldn't let me play your piano—just for a little while?"

She had to smile at his nerve. "We'll see. It rather depends if you're going to be more sensible in future and do your other work properly. People are not against you as you imagine—they really want to help, you know."

Timothy nodded. "I'll try to do better next week—thanks, Miss Price—Ouch!" he exclaimed, as Tabby dug her claws into him.

"Get down, Tabitha, immediately—Scat! Cat!" Susanna scolded.

After about twenty minutes gardening Susanna slipped indoors and phoned Graham Bryant to square things with him. He said it would be in order for the boy to stay for a while and that he would send someone to collect him at around seven o'clock.

Timothy proved to be a willing worker and it was evident that he was enjoying himself. Susanna allowed him to play the piano whilst she was preparing the tea. His playing was so sensitive that it brought a lump to her throat and she felt a thrill of pride at having such a talented young pupil.

After they had eaten he sat on the pouffee whilst she played Grieg. Susanna became so immersed in the music that she wasn't aware that Mark Liston had arrived at the cottage, or that he was standing in the sitting-room doorway listening. When she came to the end of the piece he coughed gently, and she spun round.

"I didn't want to interrupt you so I let myself in through the back door. I've been sent to fetch this young reprobate. It seems to me that instead of being punished he's been rewarded—isn't that so, Carstairs?"

"Sir," the boy mumbled, springing to his feet.

"Tea and sympathy?" Mark asked Susanna looking at the laden table.

"No, refuge from a storm," she replied

curtly. "OK, Mr. Liston, he's all yours —take him away. Actually, he's been extremely helpful; he's mowed the lawn and emptied the wheelbarrow and, what is more, he is going to mend his ways, aren't you, Tim? You see before you a reformed character. We have come to an agreement."

"Really and what's that—or mustn't I ask?"

Timothy pushed back his mop of brown hair. "Oh, I don't mind you knowing, sir. If I don't do my work properly, Miss Price won't give me my music lesson."

"I see, and I suppose this young fellow wouldn't have been playing your piano this afternoon?" Mark queried.

"So far as I am aware no ban has been placed on my piano," she informed him firmly.

Mark looked as if he were trying not to laugh. "OK, Susanna, this time you win," he said softly, momentarily forgetting the boy. His deep-brown eyes held hers and Timothy, looking from one to the other of the adults, sensed that there was something going on between them that he did not understand. Mark let the boy go out to the car and stood at the gate talking to Susanna.

"I'm coming back in about an hour's time to take you to the barn dance," he told her *sotto voce*. "I'll brook no arguments—it's my way of calling pax."

She smiled, relieved that the friction between them was gone.

"Thank you, I'd better go and get ready then." As she waved goodbye to them she realised that Mark had taken her unawares or she would probably have refused to have gone out with him.

Casting about in her wardrobe for something suitable to wear she found an Indian cotton skirt and a pretty embroidered blouse. Brushing her hair she considered leaving it loose for once, but habit made her twist it to the top of her head. She would have liked to have discarded her glasses for her contact lenses, but had taken refuge behind them for so long now that she didn't think she would feel comfortable without them, besides all the time she wore them there was less chance of Mark's realising she was Susanna Rosenfield.

"Susanna, you look absolutely stunning in that outfit," Mark told her when she opened the door to him. "Am I forgiven for our little difference of opinion about young Timothy Carstairs? Although, of course, I still think I'm right."

"And I still think I am so let's drop the subject, shall we? Tim's having a rough time and it's my responsibility to help him through it."

"You mustn't allow yourself to become emotionally involved with your pupils," he said quietly.

She picked up her handbag and checked that she had her key. "No, sir, I'll try to remember in future."

He frowned. "Oh come on, Susanna, if we allowed ourselves to get het up about every kid with a broken background we'd end up having a nervous breakdown in the first six months."

Her mouth set in a tight line. "Point

taken—now are we going to that barn dance or not?"

The village hall was packed. Susanna felt a strangely mounting excitement. Tonight she felt more like her former self than she had done for over two years. It was rather as if a metamorphosis was taking place within her, like a butterfly just about to burst forth from a chrysalis. They sat with Roger Marlowe and Amanda Bryant and some of the other staff from the school.

"You look fantastic in that gear," Roger told her as he claimed his dance and she coloured. He whirled her round until at last, breathless and begging for a rest, she sank down at one of the small tables scattered about the room. Judy, delighted to see her friend, came over to join her and they sat watching the whirling, happy villagers and enjoying the music. Susanna noticed that Mark was dancing with Amanda and suddenly she knew that she wanted him to dance with her—to feel his arms about her. Tom wove his way towards them.

"Susie—how lovely to see you!" He insisted on dancing with her and proved to be incredibly awkward, trampling over her feet and turning the wrong way. Susanna found herself laughing as she hadn't done for months. She realised that her father would be astounded if he could see the change that had been wrought in her during the short time that he had been away. The dance came to an end and Susanna returned to her seat. Suddenly Mark was by her side holding out his hand and, as if in a dream, she took it and he led her onto the floor.

"You're full of surprises, Susanna Price. Whoever would have believed that you could dance like this. I knew you'd got hidden depths," he murmured. She felt exhilarated by the music and Mark's closeness. It was a mild May evening and the doors at the back of the barn were wide open. Taking her hand he led her out into the gathering dusk. They wandered alongside the stream at the edge of the meadow. The lights from the barn spilled goldenly onto the grass and the music filled the air.

Mark's arm encircled her waist; his hand through her thin cotton blouse sent tremors down her spine. When he stooped to kiss her she did not resist, but his lips barely brushed hers, sending shivers of expectation dancing through her before he pulled away.

"I wanted to say I was sorry, Susanna, for upsetting you the other day." And, catching her hand in his, he pulled her back across the meadow in the direction of the barn. "It must be almost supper-time. They'll be wondering where we've got to."

Susanna suddenly felt as if she were walking on air. Ralph Ewart-James had finally been cast out of her life for ever. He was no longer able to hurt her.

If Judy noticed the stars in Susanna's eyes and her flushed cheeks she made no comment.

"Where have you been, Mark?" Mandy demanded, pouting prettily.

"We got hot so Susanna and I went for

a walk to cool off," he told her lightly. Roger raised his eyebrows comically and Judy said:

"Supper, everyone."

Susanna could not remember the last time she had enjoyed herself so much. She felt positively elated by the end of the evening.

"I just wonder how many I can expect in my congregation tomorrow morning?" Tom remarked mopping his brow.

It was past midnight when Mark finally drove Susanna home. He insisted on accompanying her to the front door.

"I don't feel the least bit tired. Come and have some coffee," she invited impulsively.

"Won't your Mrs. Gotobed be watching out?" he asked her laughingly.

"Quite likely, but who cares?" Opening the front door she switched on the light. She suddenly felt reckless—full of her former gay abandon. Catching sight of her reflection in the hall mirror she saw that her cheeks were flushed and her eyes sparkling.

"Oh Mark, I have enjoyed myself. Thank you for taking me."

He shut the door softly and came to stand behind her. "Show me how much," he commanded and, catching her by the shoulders, drew her into his arms. His lips came down on hers, firm and demanding, and she was swept away on a wave of emotion. His fingers entwined in her hair loosening the pins. She could feel the warmth of his body pressing against her. She had not believed she could feel like this about any man again and closed her eyes willing the moment to go on for ever, but just as suddenly, he released her.

"Wow, that was some thank-you!" he said, his dark brown eyes dancing. "I think it's a case of still waters running deep where you're concerned, Susie Price." He straightened his tie and taking her hand pulled her in front of the mirror where she laughed as she saw her dishevelled hair. He gently removed the rest of the pins so that her hair tumbled silkily over her shoulders. He buried his face in it. "I've been wanting to do that for ages. It smells like spring flowers. You'd better go and make that coffee before I lose my reason altogether. My adrenalin's going wild!"

She pushed open the sitting-room door, her heart beating like a caged bird. "Why don't you put on a record whilst I'm making the coffee?" she asked lightly, trying to regain control of herself.

"Good idea—if I dare use this superb music centre. It must have cost a small fortune. Is it yours or your fathers?"

"Mine," she told him switching on the fire. "It's quite simple to operate." She had gone into the kitchen when he called:

"Don't you like anything apart from classical?"

"Yes, of course—you'll find some modern at the back . . ." Suddenly her heart missed a beat and her hand flew to her mouth. She came abruptly back from dreamland to the present moment, as the realisation of what she had done in allowing Mark to browse through her records suddenly dawned on her. She tried to keep calm, mechanically assembling mugs, sugar, cream and biscuits on a tray. Hurriedly she made the coffee. Perhaps he wouldn't notice. Maybe he would find something he liked before he came across it. She hastened into the sitting-room. But it was too late, for Mark had found her record and was examining her photograph on the sleeve—a strange expression on his face.

"Remove your glasses," he ordered her in an oddly quiet tone.

"Why?" she asked, her heart hammering, knowing full well what he was driving at. "I can't see too well without them."

He got to his feet and took the tray from her, setting it down on the coffee-table. "OK—then let me. I want to settle this thing once and for all and as you're obviously prepared to continue with this charade . . . Unlike you, I don't forget a face. I have a very long memory."

"Mark, what are you talking about?" she asked shakily. Before she realised what he was about, he had removed her spectacles and was surveying her, head on one side. "Yes, there's no possible doubt. I think I knew the truth all the time, but I needed to make sure. You are Susanna Rosenfield, aren't you?"

There had been far too much excitement for one evening. Susanna covered her face with her hands and sank slowly onto the sofa.

"Oh, what does it matter," she said wearily. "Yes, I am Susanna Rosenfield. Now are you satisfied?"

Mark came to sit beside her. "I thought so, but I wanted to hear it from your own lips."

"So that you can write about it for some wretched newspaper, I suppose. Although it surely wouldn't make that much of a scoop," she added bitterly.

"Susanna, what are you afraid of? You've done nothing wrong, so why are you hiding?"

"I thought it was too good to last," she murmured and, getting to her feet, crossed to the window. She had not pulled the curtains and she gazed into the darkness pressing her burning forehead against the glass. "So what do you intend to do?" she asked him presently.

"Do? What do you expect me to do?" He came to stand beside her and, catching her by the shoulders, swung her round to face him. Her lovely blue eyes were bright with unshed tears.

"I don't know—but you're obviously going to do something, aren't you, now that you've found me out! Oh why can't you leave me alone?"

He moved away from her abruptly. "All right, if that's what you want—I will, but you disappoint me, Susanna."

He left the room and soon she heard the front door slam shut behind him. She picked up the discarded record she had made of the Rachmaninov piano concerto. "Oh Tim, if you only knew the heartbreak fame brings with it you wouldn't want it," and she flung herself on the sofa in a paroxysm of weeping.

4

"YOU didn't make it to morning service yesterday either, then?" Tom remarked, meeting up with Susanna outside Ravenscourt College on Monday morning.

"No, I'm afraid I overslept and then woke up with a blinding headache," she told him truthfully. He shot her a swift glance.

"Too much cider, eh?"

She forced a smile. "Something like that."

If he thought how peaky she was looking, he didn't make any comment.

Susanna's pupils had never known her be so snappy before, and even Timothy Carstairs did not escape the length of her tongue. His lack of practising was very evident and it seemed that nothing he did could please his music teacher that morning. At the end of the lesson,

106

Susanna caught him eyeing her in a way that made her realise that he must be wondering if this were the same Miss Price who had been so kind to him on Saturday afternoon.

"No more nonsense, Tim," she told him firmly. "It doesn't pay off, you see. Next week I shall expect a vast improvement—now run along."

Her heart was heavy. She had managed to avoid Mark for most of that day. He had spent the coffee-break talking to Alec and Mandy Bryant, and she had not clapped eyes on him at lunchtime. The thought of the following morning when she would be forced to face Mark, as they took the singing lessons together, made her feel quite nervous. She was greatly relieved when the end of the afternoon came at last for her headache had returned. The Head caught up with her just as she was about to leave Ravenscourt.

"Miss Price—a word before you go. We are having a meeting tonight about the entertainment for Speech Day and, as you are involved this time, I wondered if you might be able to attend. I intended asking you before, but, of course, you don't come in on Fridays. I know it's short notice—eight o'clock in the schoolhouse."

Susanna indicated the bike. "I am free, Mr. Bryant, but I'm afraid this is my only form of transport."

"That's all right—someone will pick you up, no doubt. I'll have a word with young Marlowe—will seven forty-five suit you?"

Susanna could not very well refuse. She stopped at the village store to collect a few provisions and then cycled the short distance to the cottage. Something on the doorstep caught her eye. On investigation, it proved to be a bright yellow polyanthus full of bloom. When she opened the door she found a note on the mat.

Roses would have been more appropriate, but this was all I could find round here. I'm sorry if I upset you,

Susie. Let's forget the whole episode and start afresh, shall we? Mark.

Confound him. What right had he to stir up the past and interfere in her life? She picked up the bright little plant and stood it on a saucer on the kitchen window-sill. Tears pricked her eyes and she brushed them fiercely away. Why was she so foolish in her handling of men? She fed Tabitha and then decided to go for a short walk to clear her head.

Past the cottages the village petered out ending with a few straggling farm buildings. After that a lane wound between fields for a couple of miles to the next village. Hands deep in pockets, Susanna walked along, ignoring the gathering rain clouds that made the Scots pines look ominous and black. There was a hedgehog in the road—the silly things took so long to cross that they often ended their lives that way. It looked at her with bright black eyes and she clucked her tongue at it. Reaching the hump-backed bridge spanning the little stream she leant over and idly watched a twig drifting by. In the distance she could see the thatched-roofed cottage belonging to a retired colonel. It was peaceful and until now she had been happy with this kind of existence, but now Mark Liston had come along to shatter that peace and to stir up memories of things that she was trying desperately hard to forget. How could she convince him that Susanna Rosenfield had ceased to exist on that fateful day, over two years ago, when Marcia Ewart-James had turned up at the hotel in Italy demanding to see her husband?

The first drops of rain sent Susanna hurriedly retracing her steps. She was drenched through by the time she reached the cottage, but her headache had quite gone.

After a bath she changed into her neat two-piece, ate a cold supper and listened to the radio. When a rap came on the door she picked up her handbag and went into the hall. It was Mark. They stood staring at each other in silence for a moment and then he said somewhat awkwardly:

"Roger's on duty so I've come to collect you instead. I meant to mention the meeting at the weekend, but I clean forgot."

"Thank you for the plant—it's beautiful," she said in a rush.

He smiled at that. "You liked my peace-offering, did you? I thought it was worth a try. After all, if we have to work together for the rest of this term we don't want to be at loggerheads, do we?"

"No, of course not," she muttered. "It was foolish of me to mind so much. I realise that now, but it was just the initial shock of learning that you'd sussed me out."

He waited whilst she closed the front door, and did not say anything further until they were on their way to Ravenscourt College.

"You can trust me, you know. I shan't betray your confidence. If you want to sink into oblivion, then who am I to stop you? It's a pity though—you have a lot of talent."

"I'm happier as I am," she told him. "And now let's drop the subject, shall we, Mark?"

The meeting did not take nearly so long as Susanna had anticipated and, fortunately, Graham Bryant approved the ideas put forward by Mark and herself. Afterwards the Head came to speak to Susanna.

"I intended to thank you for helping young Carstairs on Saturday, Miss Price. He's going through a difficult patch, I'm afraid, and I appreciate what you're doing for him. As a matter of fact, I've had a letter from his grandmother this morning. Tells me his mother is likely to return to England shortly, so no doubt Julia Carstairs will be down to see young Timothy."

Susanna was just about to enquire whether the affair was over between Julia Carstairs and the film director when Graham Bryant was called away to the telephone.

One of the day staff offered Susanna a lift home, rather to her disappointment, and so she did not get the chance to speak to Mark again that evening. Her heart was lighter, however, now that they had made up their differences. She realised that in the short time she had known Mark she had come to regard him as a friend and that she enjoyed his company more than she was willing to admit. His kisses had ignited a flame within her that she thought had been extinguished for ever.

The week sped by on wings. Susanna enjoyed her teaching programme and realised that for the first time in over two years she was feeling fulfilled. On Thursday, just as she was about to cycle home, there was a heavy downpour of rain.

"You're not cycling home in this," Mark told her. "Come and have some tea and then I'll drive you back to the cottage."

Amanda Bryant was in the staff sitting-room staring moodily out of the window.

She turned away and said: "Bang goes our drive, I suppose, Mark?"

"Well, I must admit I'm not too keen on taking you out in this. You've got quite enough to contend with at present without slippery roads. In any case, I've got to be back by six to take prep—there'll be plenty of other times, Mandy," he replied placating her. "Roger and I are helping Mandy learn to drive and it's my turn tonight," he explained briefly to Susanna.

Susanna paused in the act of wielding the teapot. "Oh, really, how are you getting on, Amanda?"

Amanda smiled and caught Mark's arm. "You'd better ask my teacher. He's very patient. Roger tends to get cross if I do something stupid, but Mark is so very encouraging. He really inspires confidence in me." She smiled up at him with her large green eyes and fluttered her long lashes. Susanna felt a sudden knot in her throat. She realised that she was just a little envious of this vivacious young woman. Beside her she must appear very boring company. She took a sip of tea. It was scalding hot and made her eyes water.

Alec wandered into the room. "Carstairs seems to have settled down again, Miss Price."

Susanna nodded. "Yes, he's OK for the time being. He feels secure at school and, fortunately, we get on well together."

"How I'd hate to teach," Amanda remarked helping herself to a toasted tea-cake. "You must be awfully dedicated."

"Well, you must know that saying about those who can't make the grade at anything else teaching," Susanna replied. She caught Mark's gaze and coloured.

Alec laughed. "Yes, it rather makes me wonder just how much wasted talent there is in the teaching profession. I'll bet you could have made a career out of playing the piano if you had so desired."

Susanna sipped her tea so that she didn't have to answer and Mark said, "I expect there are secret ambitions locked inside all of us if the truth be known."

About ten minutes later he got to his

feet and set his empty tea things on the trolley. "OK then, Susanna, shall we go?"

Mandy looked quite sulky, but she didn't volunteer to accompany them. Susanna felt a little tinge of some emotion inside her. It was evident that Miss Amanda Bryant was setting her cap at Mark. Well, she needn't fear competition from Susanna. After all, Amanda was attractive, leggy and effervescent. Beside her, Susanna felt like a maiden aunt. Amanda saw Mark in the evening frequently whilst she, Susanna, had to be content with the occasional lift home and shop talk. For an instant she remembered the warmth of his kisses—the way he had made her feel alive and vibrant once again. She hastily got to her feet and brushed the crumbs off her skirt, wondering what on earth had come over her.

They were nearly at Lavender Cottage when Mark said casually:

"Are you doing anything this Saturday, Susanna?"

"Just the usual shopping and household chores, why?"

"Could you skate over the housework for once and come to Brancaster with me? I fancy a trip to the sea. A bit early, I know, but who cares?"

Susanna tried not to appear too keen, although her heart nearly missed a beat. "So where's everyone else this weekend then?"

"Oh, they've got their various pursuits. Roger's on duty—the penalty of being resident. Alec is off to visit George Purbright. A group are going to Norwich . . ."

"And Mandy?" she asked, almost without meaning to.

He shot her a surprised glance. "Mandy is going to Lincolnshire to a wedding of some cousin of hers. As a matter of fact she did ask me to accompany her, but weddings aren't my scene—besides, I don't have a top hat!"

So Mark had asked Susanna merely because he wanted some company and there was nothing else doing. Some perversity within her almost made her refuse, but she realised that she would be sorry if she did.

"Are you going to Brancaster for any particular reason?" she ventured.

"Nope—just fancied a bit of invigorating sea air. I like that neck of the woods. Of course, if you'd prefer somewhere else—always assuming that you've decided to come."

She smiled up at him; her heart was doing strange things.

"Thank you, Mark, I'd like that. As a matter of fact, I've never been to Brancaster."

"Ah, well then, you've never lived. I'll give you a buzz tomorrow evening to confirm times."

"Do we need a picnic?"

"No, I know a nice eating-place." He pulled up outside the cottage.

"Would you like to come in for a sherry?"

He consulted his watch. "Love to, but, unfortunately, I've a prep to supervise at six and it's getting on that way now so I'd better take a rain-check," and he laughed and indicated the weather.

Susanna stood and waved him goodbye, grinning as she saw Mrs. Gotobed's nets twitch. She sang as she prepared her supper.

On Friday Susanna helped Judy to do the church flowers and clean the brasses, along with an army of other ladies from the parish.

"Oh, that's beautiful," Judy approved, standing back to admire the effect. "There's nothing like fresh flowers and greenery. Come back to the rectory for coffee, Susie. Tom should have hopefully finished writing his sermon by now, and I know there's something he wants to ask you. Besides, I need you for a fitting for your dress."

The dogs greeted Susanna rapturously and Tom appeared in his study doorway waving a sheaf of papers.

"I'm nearly done—give me another ten minutes or so. Fire and brimstone this week—need something to shake the congregation out of their apathy!"

"Oh dear," Susanna said. "I do hope you're not including me or I shall beat a hasty retreat."

Tom laughed. "Present company excluded, of course. Tell you what, Susie, would you play something for me whilst Judy's making coffee? Music gives me inspiration—food for thought etc."

Susanna smilingly agreed. "What sort of something?"

"Oh, Beethoven, Chopin—you choose. There's some music in the piano stall—of sorts."

"Give me a moment then." Susanna chose Chopin, but she played it from memory. She was still playing when Judy brought in the coffee and Tom emerged silently from his study. Both sat quietly on the sofa drinking in the beauty of the music. Tom caught Judy's hand in his. Susanna was in a magical world and had momentarily forgotten that she was in the rectory sitting-room. As she finished playing the polonaise they applauded and she spun round, cheeks flushed.

"You should have stopped me. I've gone on for far too long."

"Oh, Susie, that was magnificent. I've never really heard you play before. I could listen for ever," Judy said.

"Did you finish your sermon, Tom? That's more to the point."

"Oh, yes thanks. Susie, that was splendid. You're really talented, and you weren't using any music, were you?"

"Didn't you ever want to make it a career?" Judy asked pouring the coffee.

Susanna pretended to look puzzled. "I have done, haven't I?"

"Oh, you know what I mean—go on the stage?"

Susanna forced a laugh. "I don't think I'm the type, Judy. You've no doubt noticed by now that I'm really rather introvert. Now, Tom, Judy says there's something you wanted to ask me."

"Yes, indeed. Ellen informed me the other day that her sister is in a nursing home now and she'll be wanting to visit her sometimes on Sundays and so she won't be able to play the organ every week, as she has been doing. I was wondering if either you, or perhaps one of the boys—Carstairs for instance—could take a turn. I'd be deeply grateful."

Susanna was inwardly relieved. She had wondered just what Tom had been about to ask her. "Why, of course, I'm sure we can arrange something."

Judy beamed. "Well that's taken a weight of his mind, I can tell you. And now if you've finished your coffee we'll go into the other room and I'll fit that dress."

Afterwards, Judy tried to persuade Susanna to stay to lunch but she refused. "It's kind of you, Judy, but I've a million and one things to do this afternoon. Mark's taking me to Brancaster tomorrow and so I'm doing my chores today."

"You know, Susie, it only seems five minutes ago when we were all strangers, and now look how the relationships are progressing."

"Now don't go jumping to any

conclusions, Judy. It's my belief that Mark is far more interested in Amanda Bryant than he'll ever be in me. She's away this weekend, and I rather think he's in need of some company, hence his motive for asking me out."

Judy smiled. "Well, enjoy yourself anyway, honey, although I wouldn't have thought it was quite the weather for the coast. If you get half a chance bring back a few shells, could you? The boys are positively crazy about shells—some project they're doing at school."

"Have a heart, Judy, I'm sure Susanna will have better things to do than go beach-combing for you," Tom admonished her.

"I'll see what I can find," Susanna promised, patting the dogs.

It was nice to have the Davidsons' friendship, she reflected as she made her way back to Lavender Cottage. She suddenly felt extremely happy and light-hearted. Life had recently taken on a new meaning for her. She whistled a catchy tune ignoring the stares of a couple of elderly villagers chatting over their garden fence.

"Ever been to Blakeney before?" Mark asked on Saturday morning.

"No, I don't know this area at all."

He had collected Susanna early and driven into north Norfolk along an attractive stretch of coastal road following the edge of the marshes.

"A lot of this coastline is under National Trust protection," Mark explained. "A bit further on are Blakeney Point and Scolt Head nature reserves. It's an interesting area. I might see if we can bring a party of the boys here. There's bird life, and rare plants."

As they drove along Susanna gazed with interest at the stretch of salt-marshes that were brownish green in shade.

"Time for a leg-stretch, I rather think," Mark said presently. "I thought we'd take a look round Blakeney and then have an early lunch and go on to Brancaster this afternoon. How does that suit you?"

Susanna smiled. "I'm just contented to be exploring a different part of Norfolk. You obviously know this area, and yet I thought you were the new guy."

He laughed. "Yes, to Ravenscourt, but certainly not to Norfolk itself. I was born in Suffolk and my parents still live in Southwold.

Susanna was delighted by Blakeney Quay. Many yachts and small sailing-boats were dotted about in the harbour and the long channel leading out to sea, making the scene as picturesque as any postcard. Behind lay the flat fascinating marshes broken by a row of little sandhills.

"Oh, isn't it peaceful," she breathed. "It's got a soothing effect." She inhaled the tangy brine-filled air.

"It's one of the safest places for both bathing and sailing on the East coast," Mark informed her. "Now, I want to show you the Guildhall. It's fifteenth-century."

He led her into a side street and she stood gazing admiringly at the ancient building and then they went to look at the perpendicular-style church with its two towers.

"The tower at the east end is reputed to have been a beacon in years gone by," Mark said.

They wandered round the enchanting little village which was much sought after by holiday-makers who wanted a restful time. Mark took her arm. "This place attracts many artists. You get such marvellous sky effects with it being so flat in Norfolk. Of course some people find it uninteresting, but it opens up a whole new vista."

"It's lovely," Susanna enthused. She found him an interesting guide. He pointed out the flint-stone cottages explaining how they had been carefully modernised. At last he took her into the local hotel for lunch.

"This is the sort of place where one can feel at peace with the world," Susanna sighed. "It really is so tranquil."

"You're not a city lover then, I take it, Susie? Not for you the noisy city lights?"

She smiled and shrugged her shoulders. "Oh, I used to be at one time, but I've changed. I love East Anglia. It's so unspoilt and I'm always discovering something new, like today."

He rested his hand lightly over hers on the table and his eyes held hers in a searching gaze. She felt a surge of emotion such as she had not experienced since Ralph. They sat there for a few moments in silence, just enjoying each other's company, and then Mark said: "I reckon there's a lot about you, I don't know, Susanna—a lot of unanswered questions."

"Don't spoil it," she pleaded and, much to her relief, at that moment the waiter arrived with the hors d'oeuvres.

"Is it completely taboo to talk about Vienna, if we miss out all personal aspects?"

"It's an episode I've shut out of my mind. I'd rather think about the present and forget the past."

"Isn't that what nuns are supposed to do?" he queried.

"I beg your pardon?"

"I read somewhere that nuns aren't supposed to acknowledge their past. It's a void, almost as if it hadn't happened. Is that what you really want, Susie? Perhaps if you could bring yourself to talk about Ralph Ewart James . . ."

"No!" she exclaimed so violently that a couple at a nearby table looked round in surprise. "I'm sorry, it's just that it would be like rubbing salt into a raw wound. It's an episode in my life that's over and I just want to forget it. You didn't invite me out so that you could interrogate me, did you?"

He regarded her with his deep-brown eyes. "No, of course not, don't be foolish. OK, forget I spoke. Let's enjoy the present. I'll remember certain topics are taboo, but I won't guarantee never to mention them. I have an insatiable curiosity, you know."

"That's what Tom said about Judy." Susanna feeling a little ashamed of her outburst concentrated on her prawn cocktail. "So, what do people do round here when they come for holidays?"

"Oh, sail, fish—there's wildfowling too. Some, no doubt, paint or go bird-watching. It's a haven for those wanting to escape from the city." He speared a prawn. "Tell me, do you plan to stay in Bridgethorpe indefinitely?"

"I don't look into the future either," she told him, and this time there was the suspicion of a smile on her lips. "Perhaps one day I'll sell some of my compositions and retire to the seaside—somewhere like this."

"Ah, of course, you compose music too, don't you? I'd forgotten that."

"A pity you hadn't forgotten some of the other things," she said tartly, and he laughed.

She enjoyed the chicken lunch and, by the time it was over, felt completely relaxed. Mark told her about his home in Southwold and she, in turn, told him a bit about her father and her sister Catherine.

"She sounds very different from you," he commented.

"She is—totally. She's everything I'm not. She was a nurse before she married. She's extremely practical and domesticated, and a complete extrovert."

"When I first met you I thought that you were an extrovert," he ventured and she smiled.

"Yes, well maybe I've changed. People do, you know. That meal was super, Mark."

He beckoned to a waiter and asked for the bill, refusing to let Susanna pay her share. "You can treat me to some tea later on," he told her.

They made their way back down the narrow main street to the quayside where they took one final look at the sleepy little port dozing in the afternoon sunshine.

"Oh, what a good suggestion it was of yours to come here, Mark."

"And what a good idea it was of mine to bring you with me. Come on—next stop Brancaster."

Susanna leant back and closed her eyes briefly as they sped past the marshes towards Brancaster. Presently Mark manoeuvred the car into a parking space.

Brancaster met up to Susanna's expectations with its stretches of silver-gold sand. The beach was almost deserted. The bracing sea breeze whipped her hair about her face and she could taste the salt spray on her lips. Removing her sandals she ran down to the edge of the sea letting the foam splash over her feet. She turned to find Mark regarding her with gentle amusement. Stooping, he took off his sneakers and tying them together slung them over one shoulder. He pushed his socks into his pocket and then he came to join her.

The sea was like turquoise satin edged with frothy white lace. Together they walked by its side and presently he caught her hand in his. They waded out a little way, gasping as the icy water lapped about their feet.

"We could be on a desert island," she said.

"What a lovely thought. You, me and nothing but miles of golden sand and sea.

I'd like that, Susanna. I'd like it very much indeed." And he slipped an arm casually about her waist, not realising that he was sending off vibes that made her tingle at his touch.

"I promised to collect some shells for Judy's boys," she said fishing out a polythene bag from her pocket.

He laughed. "You're all prepared, I see. You were obviously a girl guide. There are some marvellous razor shells here. In fact, you have to be careful not to tread on them or you could cut your feet."

Together they scooped up some of the colourful shells lying half embedded in the sand. He held one near-perfect speciman on the palm of his hand. "Here's a marvellous example of a bivalve. Look how it makes a natural hinge."

"Nature's pretty fantastic, isn't it? It seems incredible to think that a creature lived in that—just look at all the markings on that shell." Susanna took it from him gently. "Funny sort of existence," Mark mused and she laughed.

He looked at her. Strands of honey-gold hair were escaping from the ribbon, her cheeks were flushed pink and her deep-blue eyes shining.

"You look rather like a sea creature yourself—a mermaid," he murmured. "Sometimes I don't believe you're quite real."

"Oh, I'm not—if you touch me I'll melt away into the sea," she laughingly told him, and, as he reached out a hand, she raced away across the sand. He followed in hot pursuit and catching up pulled her into his arms.

"For almost three years I've cherished a memory of a lovely golden-haired girl in a glittering turquoise dress holding a bouquet of apricot roses on that platform in Vienna. Well now I've found that girl again," he whispered and kissed her.

She caught her breath at the intensity of that kiss, for he evoked emotions deep within her. His hands caressed her sending quivers down her spine and she pressed closer feeling the warmth of his body against hers. It was as if they were alone together on their desert island. At last he released her.

"Oh, Susie, I think we were meant to meet again. You never did seem quite real to me, you know. You were like some kind of goddess glimpsed from afar."

She nestled close to him as they walked back along the beach hand in hand. Her heart seemed to be full of music— joyous, happy music. She suddenly felt deliriously happy. It was as if he had brought her back to life again.

"Oh, Mark, this is such a beautiful place," she breathed. "You know, I believe it might have been you talking about Norfolk that made me want to move there in the first place. I distinctly remember someone telling me how peaceful it was—with its unspoilt countryside and glorious skies. It made a deep impression on me at the time, but afterwards, I was never sure who had put the idea into my head. It was you, wasn't it?"

He smiled. "I suppose it could well have been, seeing how East Anglia is so near to my heart, but I must confess that I don't remember our conversation too clearly. Anyway, it's a nice thought."

"I spoke to so many people at those parties that afterwards I could never sort out just who said what."

"You lived it up in those days, didn't you, Susie?"

She sighed. "Yes, I was a bit giddy, I'll admit that, but I've suffered the consequences of my folly. I fell wildly in love with the wrong person, but I certainly didn't intend to hurt anyone—least of all Marcia."

She couldn't bring herself to go on. How well she remembered her one and only meeting with Marcia, Ralph's wife—that poor faded little woman who she hadn't even known existed.

"Mark, this is the start of a new era—all that is behind me now." She inhaled the fresh salt air deeply.

He held her close against him so that she could feel the strength of his body and smell the fresh fragrance of the soap he had used, and when he kissed her again it was as if he had set her on fire. He stroked her hair and then ran a finger down her cheekbone.

"You have the most beautiful eyes, Susanna. You should never wear glasses." Suddenly he stooped down. "One more shell to add to your collection. You won't go back into your shell again, will you, Susie? Not now that I've managed to entice you out."

She smiled up at him. "When I'm with you I have the courage to cast my shell away, but if life becomes tough then I might be forced to seek its refuge again like a hermit crab."

His arm about her waist was comforting and reassuring.

"Judy will be pleased," she said with a hint of mischief.

He raised his eyebrows. "Judy?"

"Yes, she's done everything in her power to bring us together."

He laughed. "Good old Judy. She's a thoroughly nice person. Now, are we going to get that cup of tea? All this sea air is making me thirsty."

Susanna wanted that magical day to go on for ever and was disappointed when Mark said he had to get back to Ravenscourt because he had a mound of marking to plough through. As they drove home he suddenly said:

"I wonder how Mandy's got on at the wedding today," and it was as if a shower of cold water had hit her, as the realisation dawned that Amanda Bryant had probably occupied his thoughts on more than one occasion during the day. She felt a little pang of something akin to jealousy.

Mark gave her a sideways glance. "You're not too keen on Mandy, are you, Susie?"

"Whatever makes you say that? I don't know much about her, but she seems a nice enough girl to me."

"She is when you get to know her." They lapsed into silence and presently he said: "Tired or withdrawing into your shell again?"

"A bit of both, I think," she replied quietly.

He yawned. "The sea air certainly has a soporific effect. Mind if I turn on the news? It might wake us both up listening to who's killed who, and who's planning a strike for next week."

She had to laugh, in spite of herself. "Yes, one usually knows what's going to be said. That would be one good thing about a desert island, there would be no news or worries about world affairs."

"Bliss!" he sighed. "No taxman breathing down your neck, no bills to pay. When do we leave?"

She smiled; he was certainly good company to be with. He made her feel wanted, but she realised that he probably treated every girl he dated in the same way. She should have realised that it was all too good to be true. Well the mention of Mandy had restored her to her senses just in time.

When they arrived back at Lavender Cottage Mark refused her offer of coffee, insisting that he had work to do.

"You know, I'm hooked on you, Susie," he said taking her hand between his. Her heart turned somersaults as she looked into the depths of those eyes that were like richly polished mahogany. She wished she could believe him, but was beginning to suspect that he had a silver tongue.

"Thank you, Mark. I've had a lovely time."

He pressed her hand to his lips and then leant across and opened the door for her. "We must repeat it sometime. 'Night, Susie. Take care."

He waited until she had reached the front door and then drove off, leaving her suddenly feeling very much alone.

5

JUDY brought Susanna's finished dress when she came to collect Annabel from her music lesson the following Wednesday.

"You've made an excellent job, Judy, it's really super. I hope you're going to stay and have a cup of tea with me."

"Lovely—actually, I was wondering if you might remember the name of that fabric shop in Norwich, Susie. It's slipped my memory and Mrs. Collins wants to buy some of that material—like I got Annabel—for her daughter's school dresses. I said I'd give her a ring."

"I can't remember off-hand either, but I think I've probably got the receipt in the bureau somewhere." When she had poured the tea Susanna crossed to the bureau and looked through a pile of bills. A photograph fell out and fluttered to the floor. Before she could retrieve it,

Annabel had rushed to pick it up. The little girl stared at it round-eyed.

"Goodness, Miss Price—is this you? You look fantastic, doesn't she, Mummy?"

Susanna instinctively wanted to snatch the photograph back but it was too late. It showed her on a concert platform in Vienna. She was wearing an exquisite evening gown in tones of rich turquoise and her hair fell in waves about her shoulders. In her arms she held a bouquet of apricot roses.

Judy looked from the photograph to Susanna and then back again, as if not quite sure, and then she said, "Why it is you, isn't it, Susie? You look positively beautiful—and that dress must have cost a fortune. Were you in some concert?"

Susanna turned her attention back to the bureau, so that Judy should not see how the discovery of the photograph had disturbed her. When she could trust herself to speak she said lightly:

"Oh, it was just some amateur thing, you know. Oh, good, here's the receipt."

She held out her hand for the photograph. Judy was still studying it. She wore a curious expression on her face.

"Those banks of hothouse flowers at the foot of the stage. My goodness, Susie, that must have been some amateur production."

"I like your hair like that," Annabel said stroking Tabby. "Why don't you have it like that nowadays? And you're not wearing your glasses."

"Oh, that was taken some years ago when I was rather younger," Susanna told her, and taking the photograph shut it away in the bureau.

"You possess a dress like that and yet you let me make you one," Judy said slowly.

"I could hardly wear it in the daytime now, could I? And, besides, I like this one equally as much."

Judy smiled. "Thanks, Susie, you've made my day."

"Do you really still have that dress?" asked Annabel wide-eyed.

Susanna nodded. "Yes, I do, as a matter of fact."

"Gosh, I just wish I could see it—I suppose . . ."

"Annabel!" cautioned her mother. "Thanks for the tea, Susanna. We'd best be getting along before your next pupil arrives."

Susanna went with them to the front door, Tabitha following at her heels. "If you're very good, Annabel, and practise hard, then maybe I'll let you see the dress one day."

"Now you've done it," Judy told her. "Once my daughter gets an idea into her head it's very difficult to shift it. She won't forget it, you know, she'll keep on and on . . ."

Susanna laughed. "I like to see a bit of determination. Thanks a million for my new dress, Judy. It's really lovely."

Perhaps it was time the ghosts were exorcised, Susanna thought as she returned to the sitting-room. Maybe she had shut things out of her mind trying to pretend that they hadn't happened for far too long. She hadn't worn that dress since the concert in Vienna, almost three years ago—the one that Mark Liston had attended. Suddenly she was glad that Annabel had pounced on the photograph.

The late-afternoon sunlight filtered through the conifers stippling them with gold. Mark put an arm about Susanna's shoulders and led her along a well worn track in the forest. All around them, as far as the eye could see, were misty blue-green trees. It was still and tranquil.

"You can almost feel the silence," Susanna murmured.

"Yes, it's glorious, isn't it, to be able to come here after a day's work."

"There must be hundreds of conifers here."

"Apparently Thetford Chase is reputedly the largest man-made forest in Europe . . . Look, there's a squirrel!"

She followed his gaze and smiled at the sight of the little creature scampering away amongst the tall branches.

"I suppose some people might find it a

bit sinister here, but I think it's beautiful. It's got a magic all of its own," she said.

"Ever tried composing a piece of music about it?"

"No, but it's an interesting thought. I could certainly try. There's something almost regal about those conifers."

He caught her arm and silently drew her attention to a couple of red deer gazing at them timidly from a little clearing. "Graceful creatures, aren't they?" he breathed.

A sudden noise startled them and they darted away like arrows.

"Well now that our audience has gone . . ." he said softly and she slid into his outstretched arms. His very touch sent her senses reeling. His kiss set her ablaze with longing. She wove her arms round his neck and reaching up twined her fingers in his thatch of russet hair.

"This place is enchanted, Susie. You've put a spell on it." He held her close and all around them stretched the conifers like a blue-green sea. "Oh my darling, you're so lovely, but I'm afraid I'll lose you to your composer who will come to claim you back one day."

She put a finger to his lips. "Hush, Ralph has gone from my life for ever."

The shadows lengthened dappling the trees with mysterious purple shapes. At last Mark and Susanna made their way back to where he had parked the car.

"I ought to be taking you for a candlelit supper now, but, unfortunately, I've promised to see Graham Bryant about some new English textbooks we need and then the inevitable pile of marking awaits. Who'd be a schoolteacher!"

Would Amanda be there when he went over to the Bryants' house, Susanna wondered. She told herself that if her relationship with Mark developed no further she would always be grateful to him for making life have some meaning for her again. Everything seemed brighter and more beautiful since she had known him. Each day she awakened with a renewed sense of purpose. Without realising it he had put things into perspective for her. She was not yet sure how she felt about Mark—afraid to admit to herself that she might be falling in love with him, in case she got hurt a second time round. No, she would take the best out of the relationship and try not to be too disappointed if it came to nothing more.

The phone was ringing as Susanna let herself into Lavender Cottage. It was her father. "Ah, caught you in at last. You're late home tonight. Stayed on for a staff meeting, did you?"

Susanna didn't want to discuss her outing with Mark and so she said briefly, "No, someone from Ravenscourt took me for a drive to Thetford Chase, as a matter of fact. Is everything OK your end?"

"Yes, fine." Her father outlined what had been going on in Yorkshire, but she had a sudden premonition that he was withholding something from her.

"Dad, is something the matter?"

There was a pause and then Robert Price said: "Susie, prepare yourself for a bit of a shock—or a surprise, depending on which way you view it."

Her mouth went dry. "What's wrong? You haven't decided to move to Yorkshire, have you?"

He laughed at that. "Not on your life. No, it's just that . . . Oh, if only I'd been around, but I was in Leeds for the day. Susie, this really is extremely difficult. Your aunt had a visitor at the shop whilst I was away. Someone who was looking for you."

He didn't need to say any more. Her pulse raced and there was a singing in her ears. "It was Ralph, wasn't it?"

"Yes, darling, it was."

She swallowed. "How on earth did he know about Aunt Jessie?"

"Well, apparently a friend of yours from the orchestra was holding onto some personal possessions of yours, convinced that she'd hear from you sooner or later. When she left the tour recently she handed them over to Ralph. Amongst them was a letter from your aunt and he noted the address. As he was in the vicinity he obviously decided to call and make some enquiries. I believe he's conducting in Leeds at present."

Susanna was suddenly quite calm. "I see, and I suppose Aunt Jessie's told him where I am?"

"No, not exactly, darling. She didn't give him your address—just mentioned Bridgethorpe."

"Well, that's bad enough if he's a mind to find me. I suppose this is the first time he's been in England for any length of time since I left the orchestra."

"That I wouldn't know. What will you do, Susie?"

"There's not much I can do, is there? Maybe he'll change his mind. If he comes looking for me during the daytime I shall probably be up at the school and he's got to find me first. If he does manage to track me down then I shall simply refuse to speak to him."

"Susie, don't you think you might at least try to hear him out? After all, he is divorced now."

She was astounded. "Divorced! Since when?"

149

"Darling, I thought you would have known. It was in the papers about a fortnight ago."

"Well, I didn't—not that it makes any difference. Look, Dad, I really don't want to discuss Ralph. I want nothing more to do with him. Anyway, he's got a girl-friend. In the last picture I saw of him he was sunning himself in Greece with the leader of the orchestra."

"Well, I'm sorry, Susie, that this has happened but Jessie wasn't to know what Ralph meant to you. She said he seemed a very charming man."

"Oh, he's got charm all right," she said bitterly.

"Tell you what, how about coming up here for a weekend soon," her father suggested gently.

"Yes, I might do that, Dad—when I can be sure that Ralph's clear of the area. I'm just sorry that you've had to get involved in my affairs, that's all."

After a few more moments he rang off and Susanna went into the lounge and poured herself a stiff drink. Her mind was in a complete turmoil. She had thought she was safe from Ralph hidden away here in this little backwater, but she might have known that someone as ingenious as he would find a way of seeking her out if he chose. Of course, the very fact that it had taken him this long no doubt meant that during the past two years he had been amusing himself with other women—one or two of whom she had seen him pictured with in the papers from time to time. Perhaps now that he was at last divorced he had suddenly felt a pang of conscience about her. She wondered what had become of Christabel Vernon.

Susanna supposed she could always go away from Bridgethorpe for a time until she was certain that Ralph was out of the country again, but that would mean leaving her job at Ravenscourt and Mark Liston.

She stared into the golden liquid in her glass. Should she enlist Mark's help? No, it wouldn't be fair to drag him into it all. She wondered how Ralph would react when he learnt she had another boyfriend. Well she must just stay here and face the music. She laughed. That was appropriate in the circumstances. She set down her glass and seating herself at the piano stool began to play a haunting melody that she had composed just after her break with Ralph and had seldom thought about since.

Her emotions were in conflict. She was still not sure just how much she cared for Mark or whether she really had no feelings left at all for Ralph. If he walked through that door this minute how would she react? Would she really refuse to speak to him or would she fling her arms round his neck and let all the heartache of the past years wash away? She crashed the keys fiercely, changing to a stronger tempo. Ralph had wanted to possess her body, mind and soul. She had broken free from all that. She was happy here in Bridgethorpe. No, she would not allow him to disturb her newly found peace. Her fingers flashed across the keys like lightning and Tabitha came and sat beside her.

Timothy Carstairs did not put in an appearance for his music lesson on Monday and when Susanna enquired about him Matron said darkly: "He's gone out for the day with his mother and that new fancy man of hers. That means we won't be able to do a thing with him when he returns."

"Oh, I hadn't realised Mrs. Carstairs had actually arrived in England."

Matron sniffed. "Came last Friday—didn't you see her in church yesterday listening to Timothy playing the organ, then she took him off directly afterwards."

Graham Bryant overheard the conversation. "I'm sorry, Miss Price, I should have let you know. It was very remiss of me. The problem is, as Matron so rightly says, that the boy's likely to become very unsettled again once his mother leaves. It seems that the divorce proceedings are going through and Julia Carstairs will no doubt tell him."

"Oh, dear," sighed Susanna, "just as Tim was doing so well. He played the organ beautifully yesterday. Tom was delighted."

"Yes, and in all fairness so was Julia Carstairs. She's very cooperative where Timothy's career is concerned—wants him to take a scholarship to a music college ultimately. The sad thing is that she doesn't realise the effect the breakup of her marriage is having on him. Apparently, she's got a small part in a film and will be away in America for a time, and so she's not likely to see Timothy again before the end of the term. That's why I agreed to let her take the boy out today, although goodness knows what problems we'll have to iron out when he gets back."

Susanna nodded sympathetically, inwardly dismayed by the news.

The Head frowned. "The trouble is, Miss Price, that he's at an awkward age and his grandparents find him a bit of a handful when he spends holidays with them. I suspect that, in keeping with some of our other pupils, he's really a very lonely boy. I'm sure I can rely on your support to help him over this difficult patch."

Susanna assured him that she would do all she could. Her heart ached for the boy. If only parents would realise what they did to their children when they broke up the family home.

Judy had invited Susanna in for a cup of tea after school.

"I'm glad you could come, Susie. We've just finished decorating the dining-room and I'm dying to show you," she greeted her.

Susanna duly admired the dining-room with its cream walls and biscuit-coloured carpet and gave her opinion on ideas for new curtains, and then they went into the lounge and sat chatting over tea, scones and jam. Presently James came bursting in holding aloft a tortoise for Susanna's inspection.

"Look, Miss Price, I got her for my birthday."

"Honestly, this place gets more like a menagerie every week," Judy sighed, "and now Peter wants an aviary. We spent half of Saturday night looking for a gerbil which ended up in the laundry basket—goodness alone knows how it got there. It's a wonder I haven't turned completely grey!"

Susanna laughed and Judy sent her son back into the garden. Susanna wondered if she would ever marry and have a family of her own. Until recently she had convinced herself that she did not want that any more, but since getting to know the Davidsons and seeing how happy they were she had felt strange stirrings within her. Her thoughts turned to poor lonely Timothy Carstairs and she mentioned him to Tom.

Tom stroked his chin. "Don't allow yourself to become too involved, Susie," he advised. "I know it's easy to say that, but one has to remain detached from these sort of situations, and keeping a sense of proportion is the best way of helping in the long run, believe you me."

"Don't you take any notice of him. He's as soft as putty when it comes to it," Judy said. She poured more tea. "Look, how about staying to supper, Susie? There's a good concert on TV and you don't have a colour set, do you?"

"It's awfully kind of you, Judy, but I really ought to be getting back. I've a stack of ironing to do for one thing. What is the concert?"

"*The Planets.* It's from Leeds and the conductor's that fellow with the double-barrelled name who made a splash in the paper when his divorce came up the other week."

"Ewart-James," supplied Tom. "I remember that because of the James bit."

Susanna slopped her tea into the saucer, her hand was shaking so much. She hastily set her cup down on the table and found a tissue.

Judy gave her a curious look. "Are you OK, Susanna?"

"Yes, thank you, silly of me. I appreciate your offer, but actually I do have a lot to do tonight."

"Oh, well, another time maybe. You've only got to say the word if there's anything you fancy watching in colour."

Tom reached for another scone. "I'll run you home when you're ready."

"Oh no, please don't bother. Actually I'd quite enjoy the walk, having been indoors all day." She got to her feet. "Thanks for the tea, Judy, it was most welcome."

They stood waving to her from the doorway. She supposed she ought to be thankful that Ralph's work was preventing him from making a trip to Norfolk at present, but she realised that it was probably only a question of time.

That evening Susanna toyed with the idea of watching the concert after all, but decided against it knowing that the sight of Ralph and her friends in the orchestra would only serve to stir up painful memories. Instead she tackled the ironing with great gusto, washed her hair and curled up on the sofa with a book. At ten o'clock she had just decided to go to bed when there was a soft rap on the front door, nearly making her jump out of her skin. Tabby mewed and ran into the hall. Susanna, realising that at least it couldn't be Ralph, went to investigate. The tap came again. Perhaps it was Mrs. Gotobed wanting something.

"Who is it?" she called.

"It's Timothy Carstairs," came back a rather muffled reply.

Susanna unbolted the door rapidly. The boy stood huddled on the step looking thoroughly dejected.

"Tim, I don't know what you're doing here but your explanation had better be a good one—Matron will be going out of her mind with worry—don't you realise that?" She saw the look of utter misery on the boy's face and said gently, "You'd best come in."

She took his coat and then ushered him into the kitchen.

"OK, we'll talk first and then I must think what to do about you. Tell you what, do you like hot chocolate? I was just about to make myself some."

Timothy nodded and she realised that he was close to tears.

"You must have had a job finding the cottage. It's pitch-dark out there."

"I've got a torch," he muttered.

Susanna put the milk on to boil. "Are you hungry?"

"No, I had an Indian meal. I would have prefered roast beef and Yorkshire, but that would have been too ordinary for them."

"Them?" she queried.

"My mother and Martyn." He made the name sound affected. "He's American. I guess most kids would go crazy about having an American stepfather."

"But not this one, eh?" She ruffled his hair. "So what's so very awful about him?"

"He's all swank—rolling in money and wants everyone to know it. I like my dad better. I just don't know what my mother sees in this guy." His eyes were bleak.

Susanna found some savoury biscuits and put them on a plate.

"So you're launching a protest. Is that what all this is about?"

She removed the milk as it began to froth and pouring it into two mugs mixed in the drinking chocolate. Tabby mewed and climbed up the work surface.

"Make yourself useful, Tim. Fill Tabitha's saucer with milk for me, and then answer my question, please."

"I don't want any Yankee for my step-father," he said mulishly. "I want my own father and no-one else."

"I'm afraid that sometimes what we want and what we get are two very diferent things. You can't interfere in your parents' affairs. They must make their own decisions."

He looked defiant. "They don't realise that every time I get upset I can't do my work."

"Now, you're being unfair, Tim. Your parents have their own lives to lead and you mustn't stand in their way, any more than you would want them to stand in yours. Just you remember that . . ." But, even as she tried to rationalise with him, she felt a burning resentment inside her for the way Julia Carstairs had treated her son. She replaced the milk bottle in the fridge.

"I know how you must be feeling, Tim. You're bewildered by what's going on, but in time you might grow to like this Martyn."

She found some marshmallows and floated them on top of the chocolate and then she picked up the tray.

"Come on, Tim, let's go and have supper."

She was aware that the boy desperately needed to relate to someone, but realised that it would be totally wrong of her to keep him at the cottage. She would have to phone Graham Bryant, and then what would happen to Timothy for breaking bounds? She didn't dare think of it. She had a sudden bright idea—if only she could speak with Tom Davidson first.

"You know you still haven't told me why you've run away, Tim," she ventured as the boy sipped his hot chocolate.

He traced the pattern on his mug. "No one even tries to understand how I feel about things except for you. When I got back to Ravenscourt the boys wanted to question me about the car, and what Martyn was really like, and I just couldn't stand it so I got in a scrap with Hartford junior—and then Mr. Kingsman had a go about my Maths prep. Finally, Matron bawled me out because I hadn't put my clean laundry away. I couldn't sleep and I wanted to talk to someone and so I thought of you—are you very angry?"

"No, although I have every reason to be, you know," she said regarding him solemnly. He presented rather a comical picture. In his haste to get dressed he had put his pullover on inside out; his hair was tousled and his face rather grubby.

She handed him the biscuits. "Are you really unhappy at Ravenscourt?"

He shook his head. "No, it's just when they bait me or I get bawled out for not doing my prep right."

She pushed back her hair. "You're too sensitive, Tim, that's your trouble. You must learn to take things more in your stride. Now, listen to me for a moment. Just about every job you do demands a reasonable education nowadays, and music is no exception. You want to make the grade in music—does your mother oppose you in that?"

"No—but then she doesn't really care what I do," he said sullenly.

"Which is why she came to church on Sunday to hear you playing the organ, I imagine?" She was gratified to see him colour. "Right, so let's just suppose you get a place in a music college when you're old enough—you've still got to do your academic studies. Don't you think for one moment that it isn't going to be an uphill struggle all the way. I know—I did it. Now, I'll help you all I can, but I'm not prepared to let you break rules. I'm going to ring Mr. Bryant in a moment to let him know you're safe, and when someone comes to collect you I want you to promise me that you'll not make a fuss."

She could sense him tensing up. "Can't I stay here? I won't be any trouble—I

164

promise. I just don't want to face them all. It's just that I need somewhere to be quiet for a bit."

"I'll see what I can arrange," she promised. "I bet you when you wake up tomorrow morning everything will seem that much better."

She switched on the television and then went to phone the Davidsons, praying that they hadn't gone to bed and that her plan would work.

Susanna explained the situation to Judy who, without hesitation, said that providing Graham Bryant agreed they would keep the boy at the rectory for the night. Susanna then had a quick word with Tom and left him to sort things out with the Head. She returned to the sitting room feeling greatly relieved.

"Will you play the piano for me?" Timothy demanded.

"All right, but just for a very short time," she agreed. Susanna was halfway through Beethoven's *Moonlight Sonata* when Judy rang her back.

"They'd just missed him—one of the

boys woke up, realised he wasn't there and told Matron. Graham was so relieved to know where he was that he readily agreed to us keeping him at the rectory tonight. Tom's giving me a hand to shift round the spare room now. Mark's collecting a few of Tim's belongings together and then coming to pick him up in about half an hour's time. Oh, and Susie, could you come with Tim—just to see him settled in here?" Susanna said that she would and Judy rang off.

Susanna resumed her playing of Beethoven and only when she had finished did she tell the boy about the arrangements. He nodded, obviously pleased. "I like the Davidsons. I had tea with them the other week. It'll be like staying with a proper family."

Susanna sent Timothy upstairs to the bathroom to tidy himself up. She was so concerned about his appearance that it wasn't until she went to get her coat that she remembered her own. She was wearing jeans and a rather tight-fitting sweater, and her newly washed hair fell

166

in waves down her back. Oh well, there wasn't time to do anything about it now.

"You look sort of different with your hair like that," Timothy said rather shyly, as she knotted a scarf under her chin. "Julia's got pretty hair, too."

Susanna buttoned her coat. "Surely you don't call your mother Julia?"

"She says 'Mother' makes her feel old," he told her gravely.

A few moments later there was a knock at the front door. Mark stood there looking rather grim-faced. "So where is this young reprobate? He seems to be making a habit of this." He came into the hall and, lowering his tone, added, "Got a crush on you, d'you reckon, Susie?"

"Really, Mark!" Susanna protested indignantly, and he winked at her.

She called to Timothy and he emerged from the sitting-room looking rather sheepish.

"Honestly, Carstairs, you are a clown —did you really think you could come for a late-night rendezvous without being found out?" Mark demanded.

"I'm sorry, sir," the boy mumbled, colouring.

"And so you ought to be. You can just thank your lucky stars, young man, that we didn't call the police." He jangled his car keys. "Ready when you are then, Susie."

Susanna picked up her handbag and opened the front door.

"Come along then, Timothy," Mark said, touching the boy's shoulder. "We'd better get you to your new sleeping quarters."

As they walked out to the car Susanna gave Tim a reassuring hug.

The rectory was ablaze with lights. Judy flung open the door in welcome. "Hallo, Timothy—straight upstairs and into bed with you. Have you got any pyjamas?"

"Actually," he confided rolling up a trouser leg. "I'm wearing them under here."

Mark's mouth twitched. He laid a firm hand on the boy's shoulder.

"Now, Tim, I want you to be on your

very best behaviour and to do absolutely everything Mrs. Davidson tells you—is that understood?"

The boy nodded and then turned to Susanna. "Thank you, Miss Price, for everything—that hot chocolate drink was great and the *Moonlight Sonata*," and he followed Judy up the stairs.

Mark was shaking with silent mirth. "Susie, how do you do it? I've heard of tea and sympathy, but hot chocolate and a sonata!"

Tom and Susanna joined in the joke, trying not to make a noise.

"I thought you were angry with him," she said wiping the tears of merriment from her eyes.

"Schoolteachers are extremely good actors, as you must surely have realised by now. I just never know what those boys are going to get up to next."

"Makes life interesting," Tom remarked. "Now whilst Judy's settling Timothy in, I insist on pouring you both a glass of my home-made wine."

He took Susanna's coat and raised his

eyebrows as she pulled off her headscarf rather self-consciously. "Susie, you look devastating with your hair like that, doesn't she, Mark?"

Mark smilingly assented and Susanna blushed. "I wasn't expecting to go visiting. What will happen to Tim, Mark?"

"Oh, I expect Graham Bryant will give him a lecture and then it will all blow over. Children are pretty resilient, you know. He'll soon get used to this American fellow. Probably be going out there for holidays next. We spend a lot of time worrying unnecessarily. The Head's going to ring Julia Carstairs tomorrow morning —get her to come and have a chat with him—not that it will do much good. Some of these parents need to be made to face up to their responsibilities."

Judy came downstairs just as they were embarking on a discussion about the health service. "Fell asleep almost as soon as his head touched the pillow—poor little scrap. I'm going to ask Graham if he can stay off school tomorrow."

170

"He already did today," Mark informed her gruffly.

Judy sat down on the sofa. "Well, it's all been a bit traumatic for him. He can practise the piano here and Tom can give him some Latin and collect some prep for him."

"She'll wrap Graham round her little finger," Tom informed them. "He'll have to give in."

Mark grinned. "Well, I suppose another day won't hurt. I'll admit the poor kid's been through it, but he's not to expect priority treatment every time something goes wrong."

Judy propped a cushion behind her back. "Four kids, three gerbils, two dogs. All I need is the partridge in the pear tree now!"

They laughed and Tom said, "You'll have to make do with the tortoise!"

Judy glanced across at Susanna. "Susie, you look absolutely gorgeous. Whyever don't you always wear your hair loose like that? It's so pretty, and you don't look a day older than you did in that photograph taken at the concert."

"What concert?" demanded Tom.

"Oh, just some silly thing I was playing in," Susanna said hastily.

"Talking of concerts, we watched that one that was on tonight. Jolly good too, wasn't it, Judy. That conductor Ralph Ewart-James is superb. Its apparently about three years since he last conducted in England. He's coming down to London next week. Wasn't he the fellow who was involved in some scandal with a concert pianist a few years back?"

Mark shot a look at Susanna who was sitting stock-still looking as if she'd been turned to stone, and he swiftly came to her rescue.

"I can't say I remember anything about that. Well, I don't know about you folks, but I could do with some shut-eye so I'd best run Susanna home. Thanks for all your help. Young scallywag—he's got to learn that one can't solve problems by running away from them." His eyes met Susanna's and she was forced to look away, knowing that there was a message for her in what he had said.

Mark didn't speak much on the short drive back to Lavender Cottage but as they pulled up outside, he suddenly demanded: "Did you know Ewart-James was in England?"

"Yes," she said quietly. "My father rang me up at the end of last week." She briefly filled him in on the details ending, "I suppose he'll come here eventually and, if he does, then I shall send him packing once and for all." But, even as she said it she wondered if she really meant this. The thought of Ralph filled her with a variety of emotions. She was suddenly indescribably weary. She felt extremely vulnerable and, for once, was glad when Mark declined her offer to come in. He leant over and opened the door for her.

"Well, 'night then, love. Don't lose any sleep over Tim and, if you want any help to send Ralph packing, you can count on me," and he bent and kissed her gently on the mouth.

6

JULIA Carstairs tapped her cigarette into the ashtray with long varnished fingernails. She was one of those naturally beautiful women with a creamy complexion and waving dark auburn hair.

"Tim has told me such a lot about you, Miss Price. I'm so glad we've met. You think he's got something going for him then regarding his music?"

"Yes, if he perseveres he has the making of a brilliant pianist," Susanna told her.

Julia spread her hands expressively. "Well, we only want the very best for him, of course, no expenses spared. He'll get used to Martyn given time, I guess."

Susanna adjusted her spectacles. "You see part of Tim's trouble is that he doesn't feel secure and he needs stability."

Julia Carstairs sighed rather impatiently. "Believe you me, I've heard all this before from Mr. Bryant. I appreciate your concern for him, and it isn't that we don't care. It's just circumstances. I mean, Tim's father can't have him whilst he's on a job, and Tim can't very well be with me whilst I'm filming—so surely Ravenscourt College is the best place for him?"

"Yes, during the term time, but it's the holidays we're bothered about. Isn't there anyone, apart from his grandparents, who could have him to stay with them?"

Julia considered and then said: "Martyn and I might manage to have him in America for part of the summer. If not, then I'll have to see what else I can come up with—maybe summer camp." She glanced at her wrist-watch and then got to her feet apologetically, extending her hand. "Thanks for seeing me, Miss Price, I'll be in touch just so soon as I've got something fixed up." And she drifted out of Graham Bryant's study leaving a trail of exotic perfume behind her.

Susanna sighed and picked up her note-book. The Head appeared in the doorway, as if on cue, and she told him briefly about the interview.

Mark had arranged to drive her home and was waiting in the staffroom engrossed in a newspaper. "Come on—I can see you're bursting to tell me all about it," he said as they left the college and walked towards the garages. She recounted what had taken place, finishing:

"Tom and Judy Davidson are keeping Tim at the rectory for a short while longer. I was in two minds whether to advise Mrs. Carstairs against seeing him or not, but she's arranged to pop in for just half an hour. Personally, I reckon that as soon as she's returned to America all will be back to normal as far as Tim's concerned."

"She really does sound an irresponsible young woman," Mark commented as they reached the garages. "Why have children at all if you don't intend to look after them—summer camp indeed!"

Susanna shrugged. "Well, at least she's cooperative regarding Tim's music—if

only we can help him through this difficult period."

Mark caught her arm. "Don't worry,
Susie, he'll be all right. You'll see."

Timothy Carstairs returned to school a
much happier boy. Judy and Tom promised to have him back at the rectory for
tea that Saturday. On Friday evening
Mark came to supper with Susanna.
When he had accepted her invitation he
had explained that he might be rather
late, as he had already arranged to play
badminton with Mandy Bryant at 6.30
p.m. Susanna had felt a little put out by
this and wondered just how interested
Mark was in Amanda. She went to a lot
of trouble preparing the meal, wanting
everything to be just right. She dressed
carefully in a cotton skirt and her
embroidered blouse leaving her hair
loose.

"That was a great meal, Susie," he told
her setting down his spoon. "You're the
first woman I've known who can cook,
apart from my mother, of course."

She smiled. "It was a case of having to

and, actually, I admit I enjoy it—more cheesecake?"

He patted his stomach. "I should say no, but you could twist my arm. It's delicious." He poured more wine and they sat in the candlelight. "This is bliss. No deputations from small boys to tell me that Sopwith junior has got a toothache or Rawlinson is homesick."

She laughed. "Don't you miss your old life? It must have been more scintillating than Ravenscourt College."

He leant back in his chair, suddenly serious. "Oh yes—you could have called it that—reporting on who had torn whom to pieces in which bloody battle."

"But surely it wasn't all like that? I mean you weren't always a war correspondent, were you? What about Vienna?"

His expression softened. "Ah, that was the nice side. You know, I remember that party as if it were only yesterday."

"I've got a photograph. It fell out of the bureau when I was looking for something for Judy. That's what she was refering to the other night." She fetched it and put it on the table in front of him.

"That's very good—brings back some happy memories, doesn't it, Susie?"

She nodded and, for just a moment, allowed herself to drift away into the past. It was as if she could hear the applause in that concert hall; smell the scent of those apricot roses and, afterwards, feel the warmth of Ralph's kisses. Abruptly she said: "I'd better stop reminiscing, I vowed I wouldn't."

He handed her the photograph. "Well if Ralph Ewart-James is arriving on the scene shortly, you won't be able to run away from the past any longer. Will you really give him his marching orders?"

"Oh, Mark, I just don't know. I'm so confused. Anyway, he's got to find me first. Maybe he'll get cold feet—change his mind. It's probably just that he wants to look me up for old time's sake. It's just unfortunate that Aunt Jessie told him I was in Norfolk."

"He could have tracked you down in other ways if he'd had a mind to. It beats me why he's left it so long. Anyway, tonight I have you entirely to myself. First I'm going to help you with the washing-up and then will you play part of the Rachmaninov for me?"

She began to collect the dishes together. "That's not a very good idea, Mark. We could always listen to the record."

"What, when I've got the real McCoy sitting here in front of me? You must be joking—records are only second best." He got to his feet and caught her in his arms stroking her hair and kissing her gently.

"Susie, I want you to promise me one thing."

"What's that?" she asked him softly.

"If you decide to return to Ewart-James don't forget that I exist, will you?"

"Oh, Mark, whatever makes you think that Ralph has any influence left over me after all these years? Why do you suppose I left him and haven't been in contact since?"

He cupped her chin between his fingers

and looked into her deep-blue eyes, like gentians he thought. "You've been waiting for him to make the first move. He's wounded your pride and he's got to put that right. Anyway, remember you can count on my friendship, no matter what."

Could Ralph even now have the power to spoil her relationship with Mark, she wondered. She must not allow him to come back into her life again.

Later Mark stood beside her as she played Rachmaninov. The music swelled, filling the cottage with its beauty. She played with such sensitivity that he was deeply moved. Here was a genuine artist, a girl whose fingertips possessed a magical quality. He remembered her in Vienna; she had captured the hearts of that audience with her rendering of the second Rachmaninov concerto. She had captured his too, but he was not able to admit it because she had already given her own heart to Ralph Ewart-James. Mark felt certain that Susanna still loved her conductor, however much she insisted otherwise.

Afterwards Susanna put on some records and they danced together. As he held her close, Mark wondered whether this would be for the last time.

Susanna sensed that Mark was in a strange mood that evening and wondered if it had anything to do with Mandy Bryant. Perhaps she had not liked it when he had abruptly left her after their game of badminton.

"I'm afraid this must seem an awfully tame sort of evening to you," she said suddenly. "Piano music—dancing waltzes. Perhaps I should have invited Amanda and Roger along to have livened things up a bit."

He looked at her in surprise. "I've enjoyed myself immensely. I don't go on all that modern dance routine—haven't got the energy for it for one thing! This is more my line. What's the matter, Susie?"

"Nothing—I just thought perhaps this seemed a bit of a bore to you, that's all

I haven't socialized for so long that I'm a bit out of touch."

His eyes twinkled. "You're doing just fine," he assured her and she grinned and retorted, "Perhaps I ought to try something more modern like this," and she began spinning and twirling wildly about the room. He stood watching her for a few moments and then as she whirled towards him he caught her in his arms and held her there laughingly. She was breathless; her hair dishevelled and her cheeks flushed.

"You're a mixture of contrasts, Susie, one minute sedately playing Rachmaninov and the next dancing like that. Sometimes, I don't think I know you at all!"

She laughed. "I change my mood like the weather, I know. Ralph used to say it was due to my artistic temperament." She bit her lip as she saw his expression, wondering what on earth had possessed her to mention Ralph.

Mark took her hand. "I'm sorry, my love, but I'm afraid I've got to go. It's past midnight and, as you know, I'm on

183

duty at Ravenscourt tomorrow. It's been a super evening, Susie, and you're a super girl—see you soon," and he bent and kissed her gently.

A few moments later she stood waving him goodbye, letting the night air cool her flushed cheeks. If only she knew how he really felt about her. She had told herself that she would never fall in love again, but now she seemed to be doing just that —or could it be that she was just imagining the extent of her feelings for him, because he was the first man who had shown an interest in her since Ralph?

Susanna went back into the cottage and washed up the coffee-cups thoughtfully. Perhaps it would be better if she cooled her relationship with Mark now before she became hurt. He would probably be surprised if he knew how she felt about him. She suddenly wished that she had not allowed things to develop as far as this between them, for she knew that she could not cope with any more emotional upheavals.

"Men," she said to Tabitha, as she

tipped the washing-up water away. "Sometimes I think we're better off without them!" Tabby meowed, as if in agreement.

Susanna had just come in from the garden on Saturday afternoon when there was a loud rap at the front door. The distinguished-looking man with greying hair said: "So this is where you've been hiding!"

"Ralph!" Her knees turned to jelly and she stood staring at him, as if he were a ghost.

"Well, aren't you going to ask me in?" he demanded.

For several seconds she stood with her hand on the door, knowing that she ought to tell him firmly to go away, but being unable to either find the words or the courage to do so. In the end she stepped aside and numbly led the way into the sitting-room.

He stood looking around him. "Very nice—well, won't you at least ask me to sit down? I've come all the way from Leeds especially to see you, you know."

185

"So, how did you find me?" she asked, the blood singing in her ears. "Once you reached Bridgethorpe, I mean."

He settled himself more comfortably on the sofa. "Oh, that was dead easy. I encountered the rector walking along the high street so I pulled up and asked him. I'm afraid my Rolls attracted rather a lot of attention—anybody would think that the peasants round here had never seen one before. Anyway, much to my amazement, your rector recognised me. Seems he watched the concert on Monday night. I take it he doesn't know your real identity?"

"No, he doesn't. Oh, Ralph, why couldn't you have just let things be?"

"Because, my precious, you mean too much to me. I need you, Susanna, I always have done and I guess I always will—it's convincing you that's so very difficult."

"I'll go and make some tea," she said, and he laughed.

"Tea, the Englishwoman's answer to

everything—don't you have anything stronger to offer me?"

"Not at three o'clock in the afternoon —no."

It was ironic, she thought, as she filled the kettle, that it should have been Tom who had given Ralph her address. No doubt he had imagined himself to be doing her a favour. Now she would probably be bombarded with all sorts of awkward questions from both him and Judy. She suddenly felt inadequate to cope with the situation. Oh, why had Mark had to be on duty today!

Susanna took the tea-tray into the sitting-room and decided that she would just have to tell Ralph that he was simply not welcome here and that he must go, but it did not prove to be that easy. He seemed to be perfcctly at his ease and talked at length about how he had tried to track her down when she had left Italy, explaining that her letter of resignation, sent from France, had convinced him that she had intended remaining there for a time. When he had discovered that she was no longer there he had made exhaustive enquiries about her whereabouts, but had been unable to track her down.

"I really don't know that there's any point in my listening to all this," she had interrupted him at one stage, but he took no notice.

"I want you to believe me when I tell you that I tried desperately hard to discover where you'd gone, but that I drew a blank at every turn. In the end I decided to leave it for a time. You see I was convinced that when you had eventually cooled down you would contact me."

She stared at him incredulously. "After the way you had behaved towards me you thought I would come crawling back!"

"The months slipped by and still I did not hear from you," he continued, ignoring this last remark. "Marcia and I had one final attempt at reconcilement, but we decided that things between us would never improve and at last she consented to a divorce."

"But, in between all that, there were other women, weren't there?"

"Susanna, be fair! You had walked out on me—did you really expect me to wait in case you just happened to come back? I had one or two flirtations, I'll admit, but nothing serious—no one to compare with you, my darling. I threw myself into my work, but you were never far from my thoughts. I always hoped that one day you would return to me."

She poured more tea with hands that shook. He had such a glib tongue. If only she could believe that she still meant that much to him, but after the way he had treated her, she was not sure that she could ever trust him again.

"Well, you've finally found me," she said passing him the sugar.

"Yes, I thought I'd try one last time to track you down and here I am—aren't you glad to see me, just a little?"

Susanna swallowed hard. "I haven't had time to get over the shock yet. I must say you're looking remarkably fit."

He stirred his tea vigorously. "And so

are you, my darling, although I don't care for that hair-style and those glasses don't do much for you."

"I wasn't expecting a visitor," she said sharply.

"Well, why don't you go and pretty yourself up, my love? I'm taking you out for a meal—thought we'd go to Norwich."

Ralph had always taken it upon himself to make the decisions, she reflected, and previously she had rarely questioned them; now she said:

"Just a minute, aren't you rather taking things for granted? Who said I wanted to come for a meal with you? Who said I wanted anything more to do with you? By rights I should throw you out. You've had a long journey and I've made you tea, and now I think you should leave. You can't take up from where we left off, you know."

Ralph stared at her in surprise. "Well, this is a new Susie. OK, sweetie, if that's the way you want it, I'll be on my way. I just thought that, after I'd come all this way, you might have come out to dinner with me for old time's sake."

"Ralph, you've barged in here without a single word of explanation for the way you treated me, expecting me to behave normally."

He rubbed his cheek. "OK then, we'll talk—but over a meal. You've waited this long so you can surely wait another couple of hours?"

She was exasperated. "There are nearer places than Norwich—that's at least thirty miles away. Anyway, you don't even know if I'm free to go out with you. For all you know I might have a fiancé waiting to punch you on the nose—which you richly deserve!"

He sat up at that and, just for a moment, she saw a frown etch his forehead. "Well, is there someone?"

"Yes, as a matter of fact there is. His name's Mark Liston and he's not here just at present."

"That much I had gathered—so are you engaged to him then?"

"No—but . . ." she floundered.

His face cleared. "Well, that's settled then. He doesn't have any claims, does he? So why should he object to my taking you out for old time's sake?"

Susanna gripped the arm of the chair. "It's not as simple as that—maybe it's me who's objecting to going out with you, Ralph. If you haven't realised by now that we're through and there's absolutely no point in trying to rake up the past—then what do I have to say to convince you?"

He sighed. "I get the message loud and clear, but you were saying just now that I hadn't given you an explanation for the way I behaved towards you. Let me have the opportunity to vindicate myself—even a condemned man has that chance. At least hear me out, and then I promise to go away and never darken your doors again, if that's what you really want, and I find it hard to believe that it is."

He had got her there. Was that what she really wanted? The very sight of him had set her pulse racing and made her realise that her feelings for him were not completely stone-dead—even though she'd tried hard to convince herself that he meant nothing to her any more. She made a sudden decision. "All right, Ralph, you can take me out to dinner so that we can talk, but I want you to understand from the start that it's to be a one-off thing. There's to be absolutely no idea of us picking up the threads. Oh, and Ralph, don't you dare let anyone know who I am! Everyone round here, apart from Mark Liston, knows me as Susanna Price and that's how I want it to remain."

He shrugged his shoulders. "Suits me, sweetie—who shall I be?"

She ignored both this and the tingling sensation she experienced as he caught hold of her hand, gently encircling her wrist with his fingers. She jerked away and he looked amused.

He settled back on the sofa. "I'll take a catnap whilst you go and get ready."

She knew she ought to have her head examined, but he had taken her unawares. As she got ready she heard the piano. He was playing a hauntingly beautiful piece that she did not recognise

—one of his own compositions, she supposed. A little later she went into the sitting-room and stood by his side listening.

"Nice piano this," he said without stopping. And then he added in a matter-of-fact tone, "Do you like this piece?" and played again the tune she had heard from upstairs.

"Yes, it's lovely, but rather sad."

He caught her hand. "It's meant to be —it's for you. It's called *Susanna's Song*, and I've dedicated it to you, my darling."

She swallowed hard. "But we weren't sad, Ralph, those were happy times we had together."

"Yes, 'had'—I became sad when I lost you." He sat studying her for a moment. She wore the dress that Judy had made for her and had substituted the spectacles for her contact lenses; she had left her hair to curl softly over her shoulders, caught back at the sides with tortoiseshell combs. He flicked her appreciatively with his grey eyes.

"That's my Susie—you're as lovely as

ever!" His fingers moved to the nape of her neck lifting her hair. "I'm playing that piece at the concert in London next Thursday. It will be broadcast and everyone will hear *Susanna's Song.*"

"Ralph, no! It ought to be private, just between the two of us," she whispered.

"I had thought that if I hadn't found you by then that it might just have made you come back to me." His hand on her wrist was suddenly like a vice and his grey eyes smouldered. Something was niggling at the back of her mind.

"Ralph, just where are you proposing to stay tonight?" she demanded.

He raked her slowly with his eyes, so that she felt as if he were undressing her. "Now, Susie, I didn't think I'd better push my luck too far so I've booked in at a little place up the road called The Green Man, at Trissingham. If, of course, you'd rather offer me hospitality here . . ."

"No!" she said vehemently, and he laughed. She pulled away from him, suddenly wishing that she hadn't agreed to go out with him. "I like the music,

Ralph. I'm flattered," she told him sincerely.

Tabitha suddenly appeared in the doorway and made a beeline towards Ralph. "A moggy! Susie, don't tell me you own that wretched creature! Keep it away from me at all costs. You know I can't stand cats!"

She laughed at the expression of horror on his face. "Tabitha is one of the family and she is extremely sociable so you'll just have to put up with her, I'm afraid. Now, shall we go?"

Mrs. Gotobed was having a field day and Susanna, seeing the old lady outlined against the window, waved. As she sank back into the luxurious leather seat of the pale green Rolls Royce, Susanna realised that half the village would probably be made aware of her visitor by the next day. Suddenly it didn't seem to matter nearly so much.

Ralph told her about the concerts he was to conduct during the following month and, after a while, the conversation became so interesting, as she caught up with news of various members of the musical world that she had known, that all her resolutions went to the wind, and she found herself listening intently.

"And you, Susie," he said at last, "what have you been up to during the past two years?"

"Oh nothing very exciting. I could tell you in about ten minutes," and she outlined her life in Bridgethorpe.

"What a shocking waste!" he exclaimed in disgust.

"I don't see it like that at all. As a matter of fact, it can be extremely fulfilling and rewarding." And she told him about Timothy Carstairs.

"Well, you should be a judge of how good he is, but if you want a second opinion then you could always arrange for me to hear him play."

Susanna was enthusiastic. "Ralph, would you? I've suddenly had a brilliant idea. That would explain what you're doing in Bridgethorpe. I could say that I wrote and told you about Tim and that . . ."

"Hey, steady on!" he laughed. "Isn't that going a bit far? Do you really suppose people would swallow that? No, you'll just have to admit to having known me from way back—after all it wouldn't be so very unusual. Anyway, enough of all that for now. I don't know Norwich, but someone happened to recommend a restaurant to me."

It was about the most expensive restaurant in the city. She did not argue, knowing that Ralph could afford it. She sat luxuriating in the soft lights and tasteful furnishings; her feet sank into the deep carpets. Suddenly the years rolled away and she was taking her rightful place at Ralph's side again.

It wasn't until they were on their sweet course that he began his explanation and, by that time, the effect of the lovely surroundings and the good food and wine had mellowed her so that she was more receptive. He told her how Marcia had been in a Swiss clinic recovering from a nervous breakdown when he had first met Susanna. His wife had suffered with he nerves for many years since losing her baby and being told that she could have no more children.

"And you deserted her?" Susanna asked appalled.

"Please hear me out before you pass judgement." He poured more wine. "Marcia was ruining my life—oh, yes she was! She wouldn't come with me on my concert tours, begged of me not to leave her. On the few occasions early on in our marriage when she did accompany me she complained of being bored and we ended up quarrelling. Marcia is an extremely neurotic, selfish woman, Susie and she accused me of mental cruelty!"

Susanna remembered the thin, faded little woman with the sad eyes and wondered if she could believe him. "What I find so hard to forgive is the way you deceived me," she said tightly.

"Susie, at the time I was doing it for the very best of motives, I can assure you. I knew that I'd never get to know you once you realised I was married because it would have been against your principles to have continued with the relationship, and so I asked the few people in the orchestra who knew about Marcia to keep quiet and, for a time, they respected my wishes. I just wanted a chance . . . You see, I reckon I fell in love with you the moment I set eyes on you, and I wanted you more than anything in the world. Everything was all washed up between Marcia and me."

Susanna played with the stem of her glass. "And what exactly were you proposing to do, Ralph, persuade me to live in sin or commit bigamy?"

He winced at the tone of bitterness in her voice. "Susie, oh my darling, I know how it must appear to you, but believe you me, I thought that once we were engaged and you realised that I loved you enough to marry you then you'd trust me when I told you about Marcia and wait for me until the divorce came through."

She pleated her table napkin absently. "Instead of which it had the opposite effect. If only you had been straight with me right from the beginning, Ralph, but the way you treated Marcia and myself was both humiliating and callous. What hurt most of all was to realise that other people had known the truth all along—I felt a laughing-stock."

He gulped down his wine. "Susie, I see now that it was wrong of me to deceive you, but at the time it seemed the only solution. How could I have asked Marcia for a divorce when she was in that frame of mind? She wasn't prepared to listen to reason. I was so afraid that I would lose you to someone else—so jealous of any other man who dared to look at you because I loved you so much."

He sounded so very convincing that she almost began to sympathise with him. The wine had dulled her sense of reasoning. Looking at him now across the table she began to weaken.

"Poor Ralph, you certainly made a pretty tidy mess of things, didn't you?" she murmured. "It was such a terrible shock when Marcia appeared out of the blue like that."

He passed a hand across his forehead.

"Don't you think it was a shock for me too? I had absolutely no idea that she was coming. Of course it was one of my so-called friends whom I'd confided in who had given me away. No, don't ask me who, I'd rather not say. In a moment of madness I had mentioned that we were secretly engaged."

"Ralph, if only you'd been honest with me," she said gently.

"Yes, I suppose I should have taken a gamble—laid my cards on the table, but I hadn't the courage. It's ironic, but Marcia was precipitated into wanting a divorce shortly after you'd gone, after a very brief and disastrous attempt at a final reconciliation. It took so long because I'm afraid she returned to the clinic for a time. Anyway, all I can do now is to ask your forgiveness, my darling, for the way I've behaved towards you." He took her hand.

"There was my career you know, as well," she told him.

"Oh, Susie, Susie! That's digging the knife in too deeply. You could have joined another orchestra. The world was your oyster at that time—don't blame me for ruining your career. I can't bear that —don't you think I've suffered enough as it is?"

He ordered coffee and liqueurs from a hovering waiter who Susanna suspected was probably deeply interested in the conversation. She said quietly: "Don't you understand, Ralph, that for a time you killed the music inside me stone-dead? That was how it affected me. Some people—like Timothy Carstairs—get solace from their music, but at that time it was as much as I could do to take in pupils. Gradually the pain has eased and now I live for my music again, but that is only a part of it. Now I enjoy helping others to create it, although that's difficult to explain."

He refilled his glass; she noted that he was drinking rather a lot, but thought it best not to comment.

"You've changed, Susie. You're more serious—there's a maturity about you that wasn't there before." The waiter brought their order.

"So tell me about this boyfriend of yours!" Ralph demanded suddenly.

"He's called Mark Liston and he teaches at Ravenscourt College," she told him briefly and then she added, "As a matter of fact he used to be a journalist." She mentioned Vienna and his face darkened.

"I don't admire your taste—you know my opinion of journalists. How long have you known him?"

She hesitated fractionally. "Since Easter."

His eyes crinkled up with amusement. "Susie, that's barely two months. Well, he's not much competition! Won't you consider starting afresh now you've heard me out, my darling? I won't rush you, I promise. I'm going to Paris for three weeks when I've finished in London and then I'm to return for a charity concert— just about in time for your birthday, eh?"

Her heart was racing; it would be so easy to take up the relationship from where they had left of—to pretend time had stood still and all this had been a bad dream—and yet she was no longer sure that she loved Ralph. Memories of Mark Liston kept getting in the way.

"It's not as simple as you make it sound, Ralph. You can't expect to come waltzing back into my life and to pretend that nothing has happened. Quite apart from that my whole life-style is so different now that I'm not sure that I want to change it."

His eyes smouldered. "Susanna, you're talking nonsense! Of course you'd change it for what I'm offering. I'm a rich man and I'd give you the moon if I could. Susie, you're wasted shut away in that little backwater. I could make you someone again. I guarantee you could make a magnificent comeback—it's not too late." He looked around for the waiter. "I need a whisky."

"Ralph, do you think you ought to? You're in England now and there is such a thing as a breathalyser—unless, of course, you'd like me to drive the Rolls!"

He swore softly, but to her relief he took her advice and ordered a black coffee. After leaving the restaurant they walked arm in arm through the city streets stopping now and then to look in the lighted windows. For the first time in almost two and a half years they talked of that last tour together.

Later as they drove back rather fast along the narrow country lanes he said: "I have to be in London by four o'clock tomorrow for a rehearsal. What time shall I pick you up?"

She took a deep breath. "Ralph, I told you that this evening was to be a one-off thing to give you a chance to explain things."

He seemed not to hear her. "You could of course come to London with me. There are several of the old crowd still in the orchestra and they'd be delighted to see you. You could sit in on the rehearsal. It would give you the feel of things again. You could hear us rehearsing my new compositions including *Susanna's Song*."

The temptation was almost overpowering. It took a lot of will-power for her to refuse. "No, Ralph, I really couldn't bring myself to do that. I don't want any publicity—besides, I've just remembered that I'm playing the organ in church tomorrow morning."

"You're what!" he almost shouted. "Susanna Rosenfield playing the organ in church!"

"I've told you, Ralph—I'm no longer Susanna Rosenfield. I'm just plain Susie Price. Oh, why can't I make you understand?"

"Because it's so ridiculous, that's why," he said angrily.

"Well, I suppose you could always come to church. You've promised to hear Timothy Carstairs play and I could introduce you to the Head and fix something up with him."

"Susanna you must be out of your tiny mind—no way will you get me listening to you playing *All Things Bright and Beautiful*, when you're capable of so much more."

"OK, suit yourself then. I guess we'd

best say goodbye tonight," she told him stiffly.

His grip tightened on the wheel and his face bore a set expression.

"Yes, perhaps that really would be best after all. You disappoint me, Susanna. You've changed."

"Perhaps your memory of me has just dimmed," she said quietly and then, suddenly contrite, she begged, "Oh, Ralph, let's not quarrel. I can't let Tom Davidson down—not at the last moment. Perhaps I could see you for half an hour or so before you leave—if you really won't come to the service."

"You know my views on religion," he told her. "You'll have to direct me from now on—I've no idea where we are."

It was late when they finally reached Bridgethorpe and she had thought he would just drop her off at the cottage, but he insisted on accompanying her to the door. As she fumbled for her key she was suddenly filled with apprehension. He followed her inside and caught her in a tight embrace.

"I've been waiting all the evening for this," he murmured huskily and then he kissed her with a passion that was almost frightening in its intensity. He deftly unzipped the back of her dress and his hands slipped inside, moving over her body; carressing her soft skin. Her head span dizzily and then suddenly, regaining her senses, she fought him like a tigress, pushing him away from her. He looked hurt and bewildered.

"Susie, what's wrong?"

"You can't just expect—after two years . . .Oh, Ralph, I'm not sure how I feel about you any more," she said brokenly.

He held out his arms to her. "Oh, my darling, forgive me, I told you I wouldn't rush you and then I behaved like a fool, but you see I need you so badly."

She swallowed hard and fastening her dress said: "I think you'd better go, Ralph. It's been a lovely evening and I'm glad you've been able to explain things to me at last."

He took her hands gently in his. "Susie, darling, don't let this be the end because I couldn't bear it. I had hoped that tonight would be a new beginning for us both—a fresh start. Don't be hard on me, please, my love. I'll hear that boy play—anything, just so long as you don't leave me again."

Susanna fought with her emotions. "Ralph, I'd certainly like you to hear Tim play. I could do with a second opinion, but I don't want him to be a scapegoat."

Ralph smoothed his hair. "OK, we'll sort something out, although I really don't have the time tomorrow. I'll see you before I go, won't I? What time does your church service end?"

She was doing this for Tim's sake she told herself. "About 11.15 a.m."

"Right, I'll be there; we can have about an hour." He kissed her again, tenderly this time. "Good-night, my darling. I'm so glad I've found you again."

She stood and waved him goodbye filled with a mixture of emotions. When she went to bed she lay awake into the early hours her mind in a complete turmoil. She realised that she should have been firmer and told Ralph never to come to Bridgethorpe again, but it had not been that easy. Now that she had seen him again and heard his explanation she somehow felt differently towards him. Some of the bitterness had ebbed away. She tossed and turned and finally fell into a deep sleep.

7

SUSANNA had hoped to slip unobtrusively out of church after the service the following morning, but Tom waylaid her in the porch and congratulated her on her organ playing.

"Susie, that really was quite splendid. We particularly appreciated the Bach—an unexpected treat!" He shook her hand warmly and then said with interest, "It looks as if your—er—friend is admiring our graveyard—not a churchgoer himself, I take it?"

"No," she said shortly. "If you'll excuse me I'd better go. He's returning to London presently and I have to say goodbye."

Ralph was avidly studying one of the tombstones. He smiled as she caught up with him. "Ah, good-morning, Susanna. I've been standing here listening to you playing for quite some time. I approved of the Bach. Glorious morning, isn't it? Won't you change your mind and drive down to London with me? We could stop somewhere for lunch on the way."

"No, thank you, Ralph," she said firmly. "It's a nice idea, but it really isn't on. Could we go now? I think we're attracting attention—or rather your car is. Did you have to park it so close to the churchyard?"

He grinned and took her arm. As luck would have it they reached the lych-gate to find the Bryants together with Mark, still chatting to Judy. Susanna was forced to introduce them to Ralph.

"This is a friend of mine—Mr. Ralph Ewart-James. Ralph, this is Mr. Bryant the Headmaster of Ravenscourt College where I teach and his wife and niece. Mrs. Davidson is the rector's wife—and this is Mark Liston, one of my colleagues."

Cynthia Bryant was gazing at Ralph unable to conceal her astonishment. "Forgive me, but aren't you *the* Ralph Ewart-James—the conductor?"

Ralph inclined his head and then shook her hand graciously.

"I'm gratified that you should have heard of me. It's quite some time since I was last in England."

Susanna swiftly turned to Graham Bryant. "Mr. Ewart-James has kindly offered to listen to Timothy Carstairs playing so that I can have a second opinion."

He looked somewhat surprised. "Really, that would be much appreciated. I suppose you met Miss Price in connection with her musical studies?" he asked Ralph.

"You could say that," Ralph conceded.

Susanna noted that Mark's face was expressionless and wondered what he was making of the situation. Judy, on the other hand, looked positively stunned. "Would you all care to come in for coffee?" she asked brightly now.

"It's kind of you, Judy," Susanna said hastily, "but Ralph has to leave in a short while because he has a rehearsal in London this afternoon."

Ralph gave Judy a captivating smile, "Another time, perhaps, Mrs. Davidson."

Mark shot Susanna a look which spoke volumes and her heart sank for he had obviously misconstrued the situation.

As soon as they got into the car Ralph said triumphantly:

"You were having me on, weren't you, Susie? That fellow's not your boyfriend at all, or, if he is, he's certainly got a funny way of behaving towards you—just look at him now with that girl."

"I've told you that's Amanda Bryant—the Head's niece."

"So, what difference does that make? Oh come on, Susanna you'll have to try harder than that if you want to fool me," Ralph retorted, and she was aware of how it must appear to him.

When they arrived back at the cottage Susanna made some coffee and suddenly they had nothing to say to each other. The events of the past day had been so rapid that Susanna felt emotionally drained.

"Play for me, Susanna!" he demanded suddenly. "I want to know if you still have magic in those fingers. Come on, I've a project in mind for you."

She obeyed him, nervous at first and then, gaining more confidence, playing some of her own, as yet unpublished compositions, longing for his approval and at the same time afraid. She had had no professional opinions of either her playing or her compositions since she had left the orchestra.

When she had finished he snapped his fingers and said: "You'll never lose your touch, Susie—you're magnificent, my darling! Church organ music, lessons to schoolchildren—Susanna you're throwing yourself away! Do you want to hear my idea?"

She nodded and came and sat beside him on the sofa. He took her hands in his. "Susie, I've agreed to conduct a charity concert when I return to London next month. I want you to play at that concert."

She stared at him uncomprehendingly

for a moment and then, as the full impact of what he had said hit her, exclaimed vehemently:

"No, Ralph! No! I have vowed and declared that I will never play in public again."

"Susanna, we need you," he implored her. "We've lost one or two members of the orchestra recently—including our pianist—and gained some new blood. We could benefit from your talent and experience right now. You and I worked so well together in the past . . ."

She was trembling. "But you must have a pianist already at this stage."

"Only one who won't be offended if I asked you to take his place. It's Ivor Kavanagh."

She smiled. "Ivor—oh, Ralph, I'd almost forgotten Ivor."

"He's just stepped into the breach for a temporary period, but you know his heart's really in the composing side of it. This would be a golden opportunity for you to make a sparkling comeback. You could do a concerto. Everyone in the orchestra would be delighted. Darling, please do it—for my sake." Ralph got to his feet. "Look, I'll ring you before I leave England. I'll give you time to think it over. It will take courage, I know, but I also know that you can do it. And now, reluctantly, I must go."

He swept her into his arms, covering her with kisses in a sudden torrent of passion that set her on fire. "Oh, Susie! Susie! And then you say it's all over between us—are you so very sure, my darling? Isn't it just beginning for the second time round?" And she was unable to refute it.

Long after he had gone she sat staring out of the window as if in a trance. She no longer seemed to be in possession of her senses. Ralph wanted her to make a comeback as Susanna Rosenfield—to rise like a phoenix. He had always spurred her on in the past and was prepared to do so again in the future. He had faith in her.

In the garden the lilac had burst into bloom and a blackbird sang gustily in its branches. Susanna was keyed up and unable to settle to anything. She couldn't be bothered to cook lunch and made do with bread and cheese and more coffee. Suddenly she wanted to talk to Mark. He would help her to get things into perspective.

Alec answered when she rang the college. It seemed an age before Mark came on the line. She was suddenly nervous, aware of what he must be thinking, and she said in a rush, "Mark, could you possibly come over this afternoon? I'd like to talk with you."

"I've arranged to take Mandy for a driving lesson at four so there won't be too much time," he informed her brusquely. "I could come for about an hour right now if that's any good." When she said that it was he abruptly replaced the receiver.

She felt irrationally hurt for he didn't seem interested in what had taken place between her and Ralph, and had obviously made his own conclusions.

Mark arrived about a quarter of an hour later. "It's much too nice to stay in

—we'll drive to Knettishall Heath," he announced.

"Mark, I wanted to explain . . ." she said awkwardly as they set off.

"So far as I'm concerned there's nothing to explain. You've evidently made your decision. It was all pretty predictable really."

"I don't know what you mean," she said in surprise.

"Look, let's stop playing games, shall we?" he rejoined curtly. "Tom told me before church about Ralph Ewart-James' arrival yesterday. It was obvious that Tom had no idea that there was anything between the pair of you—just thought it was a casual acquaintanceship. When I saw you with Ewart-James this morning I realised you'd decided to give things another go. I suppose I ought to be happy for you."

"But, I haven't even told you what happened," she protested.

"You don't have to—that's your affair, but it's patently obvious that you didn't slam the door in his face when he appeared at the cottage as you'd threatened to do, and, from your conversation with Graham Bryant, I gather that Ewart-James is returning in the not too distant future."

"To hear Timothy Carstairs play, yes. Ralph offered to give a second opinion, and I don't want to ruin the boy's chances."

"Oh, Susanna, how could you use that as an excuse!" he reproached her. "Can't you see through him? I would never have believed you could be so gullible after the way he treated you."

"It's not like that," she assured him. "Ralph explained things to me over dinner last night—perhaps I was too impulsive racing off like that without giving him a chance to justify himself. Oh, Mark, I so badly need your advice."

"If you wanted advice then you should have rung your father, not me—I can only tell you that it's your life and you must do whatever you think fit," he said harshly.

She was bewildered; she had wanted to

discuss the situation with him, but he wouldn't even hear her out. They lapsed into silence and Susanna stared unseeingly out of the car window. Did she really know her own mind? The shock of seeing Ralph again had brought so many memories flooding back. The temptation to make a comeback at the concert, to take up again from where she had left off, was overpowering. As for any rekindling of her former relationship with Ralph she dared not think about it and only time would tell. If only she knew how Mark felt about her; she was so confused emotionally.

When they arrived at the heath Mark parked the car and they got out for a walk. It was a beautiful spot, wild and peaceful. The sun gilded the bracken and gorse bushes with gold. After a few moments Mark said:

"Susie, if you're trying to tell me that you and Ralph are back together again, then fine—you've no need to explain. It was on the cards, wasn't it? After all you left him, not the other way round, and now that he's got a divorce . . ."

"Oh, Mark, you don't understand—it's not like that. It's just that—well, he wants me to play in a charity concert he's conducting in London next month. He says I could make a comeback . . ." She trailed off as she saw his look of utter disbelief.

"Well, I've got to hand it to him. That fellow certainly knows just what to do to get you eating out of his hand, doesn't he? So what charity is it in aid of?"

She looked uncertain. "I—I don't really know."

"You don't know? Oh, come on, Susie. He's certainly a clever, calculating man, your Ralph Ewart-James, isn't he? I'm surprised at you, Susie. You're not interested in the fact that it's a charity concert, are you? It's just that it's a way of getting back in the public eye—a boost to your ego."

She was shocked. "Mark, whatever are you insinuating?"

"It wouldn't matter to you if it were a

concert to promote the protection of bats, would it? It's the fact that Ewart-James has offered to let you make a comeback that's the attraction, isn't it? You vowed you never wanted to set eyes on him again and that you'd never play in public as Susanna Rosenfield any more and yet, after just one meeting with him, he's got you grovelling at his feet and you've totally changed your mind. I only wish I knew what his secret was because he's obviously magnetised you."

She was both hurt and angry. "You kept trying to get me to talk about Ralph and now that I've finally asked you to share my confidence you don't want to listen and insult me into the bargain. As a matter of fact, I hadn't finally decided to play in that concert, but during the past few moments, I've made up my mind. Ralph is going to phone me at the end of the week and, when he does, I intend to accept his invitation. I want you to know that you're wrong about my motives, Mark. I'm not going to play in that concert to boost my ego, but to prove to myself that I can face up to situations, and that I'm not an escapist. I'm going to put the past behind me and start afresh. Oh, why can't you understand?"

He stooped to examine a plant. "Well, I just hope you're not intending to leave me in the lurch with the Speech Day concert on my hands, that's all."

"Of course not, what do you take me for?" she demanded indignantly. "My concert is the previous weekend and I don't intend to go to London until the Friday, so you certainly needn't worry on that score."

The air was like wine; the sun shone radiantly down from a cloudless azure sky striking the grass with gold. At any other time she would have been happy.

"Well, I suppose that's one consolation," Mark said tightly. "You asked for my advice earlier on so I'll give it—I think you're making the biggest mistake of your life to go rushing back to Ralph Ewart-James. He's a playboy and when he's finished using you he'll throw you over just like all the others."

"Oh, what do you know about it!" she threw at him angrily. "How can I make you understand? Anyway, quite apart from me there's Tim Carstairs to consider. I can hardly refuse Ralph's offer to hear him play, can I?"

Mark did not reply. He had stung her deeply and she averted her head so that he would not see the foolish tears which blurred her vision. She let him get ahead of her, fumbling for her handkerchief. She had thought they were friends; had genuinely believed that he would have been glad that she had the chance to play in another concert, but his accusations had wounded her. He glanced round, saw that she was distressed and walking back to her side caught her arm.

"I didn't mean to upset you, Susie. You're overwrought. It's all the excitement of the past twenty-four hours—everything happening at once. If I've seemed a bit harsh it's only because I care about what happens to you, please believe that. You must do whatever makes you happy. I won't stand in your way. It's just that maybe I find the situation hard to accept—that's all."

She couldn't trust herself to speak and blinked fiercely, struggling to gain control, knowing that it would not take much for her to break down completely. She valued Mark's friendship and wanted him to have a good opinion of her. She was quite sure now that he had never intended their relationship to blossom into anything deeper and, for that reason, would never want him to learn how much she had grown to care about him.

They came across a ruined church overgrown with ivy and a variety of weeds. "I've never seen so many churches as in Norfolk," Mark told her as they stepped through an archway. "Many of them, like this one, have just fallen into disrepair. Once upon a time they had thatched roofs —now they've got the sky for their ceiling —must be a paradise for wildlife."

Ralph did not like the countryside; he preferred the city. There would be no peace and tranquillity in his world. It would be all hustle and bustle. She would have to come to terms with that again if she decided to resume her former life—continually dashing from one capital to another; living out of suitcases, having no real home, rehearsing for hours on end until she was dropping from sheer exhaustion.

The sun shone through the glassless windows of the church. There was a rustle as a bird scurried away in the undergrowth. Mark took her hand.

"Susie, I want you to be happy. Please realise that, but you must make your own decisions."

"Oh, dear God, what shall I do?" she asked silently in her heart. If only Mark had once indicated that he loved her just a little, but he had never mentioned the word love, whereas Ralph—Ralph had proclaimed his love for her loud and clear from the rooftops.

Mark smiled suddenly. "It's peaceful this place, isn't it? There's a certain atmosphere here—a kind of timelessness. When you're famous again, Susie, I shall be able to say, I once knew Susanna

Rosenfield. We used to teach music together, you know." He kissed her gently. "I wish you all the very best, I really say that from the depths of my heart, Susie." For a moment his brown eyes held her midnight blue ones until she was forced to look away.

"So how long have you known Ralph Ewart-James?" Judy asked wide-eyed with interest. She had called to see Susanna early on Monday evening on the pretext of bringing her a jar of lemon curd, but Susanna realised with gentle amusement that it was really because she was agog with curiosity.

"Oh, I've known him for several years, as a matter of fact. I got to know quite a number of people in the musical world during my time at the Royal College of Music." She hoped Judy would be satisfied with this answer. She wondered if she ought to tell her friend the truth about herself there and then, but decided that there would be time enough for that when the arrangements for the concert were finalised.

"But you didn't mention that you knew him when we talked about that concert last week," Judy persisted puzzled.

"No, because I didn't realise then that he would be coming to see me. I'm not too keen on name-dropping for the sake of it." She realised that she must have sounded a little sharp and added, "Ralph was in the area so he decided to look me up. I took the opportunity of asking his advise over Timothy Carstairs."

"Yes, it would be lovely if the boy was able to take up a musical career."

"Well, I certainly intend to do everything to help him on his way. More tea, Judy?"

Judy passed her cup. "Yes, please, I've got an extremely sore throat today."

"Oh, you're not sickening for something, are you?" Susanna asked in concern.

Judy sneezed. "I hope not, but I've got a horrid suspicion that I'm in for a cold. Several of the parishioners have got that wretched flu-type bug and Mrs. Baldwin was coughing and spluttering all through the women's fellowship meeting. To tell you the truth, Susie, I don't feel quite A1." Susanna sympathised and Judy sipped her tea. "I see Mr. Ewart-James is conducting three concerts in London this week—one of them later this evening, but they're not being televised."

It was obvious that Judy was intent on pursuing the subject. "No, well there really isn't any need to televise a concert, in fact, I often think it can be distracting. It's the sound that's important, after all."

Judy blew her nose. "He's doing two classical—Mozart and Schubert, I think —and one of modern composers' work including some of his own. Will you listen to them?"

Susanna thought of Wednesday when the orchestra would be playing *Susanna's Song*. She realised that Judy was regarding her curiously.

"Oh, sorry, I was miles away—yes, probably—if I can."

Judy left shortly afterwards saying that

she was beginning to feel rather unwell. Susanna saw her to the gate and then went back indoors and rang her father to tell him her news. Robert Price was enthusiastic about the concert.

"It's obviously Ralph's way of making amends—rather late in the day, I agree, but still . . . It will take courage, Susie, but if you ignore this opportunity then there might never be another one. Do it for my sake, eh, Susie!"

"If you put it like that then it would be mighty difficult for me to refuse," she laughed.

"It would be lovely to think you might be about to resume your career again, darling."

"Now, Dad," she warned him, "don't you go jumping to any conclusions. This concert will quite likely be a one-off thing so that I can prove to myself and everyone else that I am still capable of playing in public—that I'm not an escapist. Quite apart from that, it will stop all the speculation once and for all and let people know that I am still very much alive. Yes, of course it will help me to decide about my future, but please don't imagine that this is an indication that I'm going back to my old life. I just don't know about that. Actually, I quite like it here in Bridgethorpe so we'll just have to wait and see what evolves. If you get the opportunity do listen to Ralph's concert that's being broadcast from London on Wednesday night. He's conducting some new compositions including some pieces of his own. One of them is dedicated to me—he's called it *Susanna's Song*."

"Well, I suppose he must still care about you, if he's gone to those lengths," Robert Price said and then added, "Susie, now that you've seen Ralph again—what are your feelings?"

"Don't ask me that yet, Dad. I haven't had time to sort myself out. Everything's happened so very quickly that I just don't know what I feel."

"Yes, darling, of course—forgive me. Just so long as you don't get hurt again," he told her gently.

"I've had my fingers burnt once so I'll

be more careful this time," she assured him. "Now, enough of me—how are things in Yorkshire?"

Robert Price informed her that although it was taking a long time, her uncle's affairs were gradually being put in order and that Aunt Jessie had finally decided to sell the business. He reckoned another month or so would just about tie matters up.

"So you should be able to come to London for the concert?" Susanna asked.

"Yes, darling, of course I will—wild horses wouldn't keep me away, besides, you'll need some moral support. What will you play?"

"Dad, you're rushing me! I've hardly had a chance to get used to the idea yet, let alone think about a programme."

"This could prove to be the turning-point in your life, Susie."

"Oh, Dad, it's only a charity concert," she reminded him and then, as she remembered Mark's words, her cheeks burned. They went on to discuss the arrangements for her half-term holiday which she had decided to spend in Yorkshire.

After she had put the phone down, Susanna went into the sitting-room and played the piano for about an hour, trying out some of her own compositions. Afterwards she felt much more relaxed and ready to face the world.

Susanna encountered Tom in the village stores the following day. He waved a shopping list at her. "Hi, Susie, I'm purchasing a few things for Judy. I'm afraid she's gone down with a streaming cold. The trouble is she's inclined to get asthmatic. Unfortunately, it's a very full week for me. I'm away tomorrow afternoon and evening at a meeting in Norwich and won't be back until late."

Susanna did some rapid thinking. "Not to worry, Tom. If Judy's still poorly tomorrow then I can get the children's tea and stay until you get back from Norwich to give her a rest."

"That's a kind thought, Susie, but what about your piano lessons?"

"One of my evening pupils has already

cancelled due to illness. I could give Annabel her lesson on Friday and I'm sure Mrs. Jenkins won't mind having hers then too—she's very amenable. If I switched some of my other pupils' times around a bit I could finish at five, which means I could be at the rectory by half-past."

Tom looked relieved. "Oh that would be a help. Thank you, Susie. Now if only I can decipher Judy's writing, I can get this shopping!"

The rehearsals for the Speech Day concert were progressing quite well and Susanna was reasonably pleased with her efforts. During breaktime on Wednesday, a worried-looking Tom told her that Judy was still unwell and that he had persuaded her to stay in bed. He was going home at lunchtime and Susanna promised that she would be at the rectory from five thirty until he returned from his meeting.

Susanna was glad of the opportunity to keep occupied as she did not want to have time to dwell on either Ralph or Mark. It was not until much later that she suddenly remembered Ralph's concert. Oh well, perhaps Judy wouldn't mind her listening to the radio.

Susanna thoroughly enjoyed her evening at the rectory. When she arrived she found Judy propped up in bed feeling a little better. The Davidson children thought it a novelty having Susanna to look after them. Whilst she cooked their tea they chattered away like magpies, showing her where things were kept and helping her to set the table.

Having cleared up the kitchen Susanna chivvied the boys into doing their prep and then tidied the lounge. She was tackling a pile of ironing when Peter came to tell her that his mother wanted to speak to her.

Judy smiled at Susanna as she entered the bedroom. "I've had a lovely sleep and I'm really feeling much better now. You're an absolute angel, Susie! The boys tell me they had a lovely supper. Now, that concert's due to start shortly, isn't it? I missed Monday night's in the end and

I do so want to hear the new composers. Are you coming to listen with me?"

Susanna consulted her watch. "There's twenty minutes yet before it begins, so I'll just finish what I was doing downstairs. Can I get you anything?"

"No thanks, I really enjoyed what I had for my tea. Right, now Annabel had her bath when she came home from school tonight, and so if you could just chase her to bed and the boys in the general direction of the bathroom saying the words 'ears and necks' to them rather loudly then I'd be very grateful. Oh, and tell them to come and say good-night when they're ready."

Susanna laughed and said that she would carry out Judy's instructions to the letter. She was beginning to have a little taste of the type of life Judy must lead and that was to say nothing of parish affairs.

A little later on she settled back in the armchair in Judy's bedroom to listen to the concert. The compositions were scintillating and fresh. Susanna tried to imagine the scene in the concert hall.

"I'd like to be there," Judy said, echoing her thoughts.

"Not tonight you wouldn't!" Susanna propped up her friend's pillows and poured her another glass of orange juice.

Judy looked at her bedside clock. "Tom should be back before too long. It's made an awfully long day for him, and for you, too."

"I've enjoyed it," Susanna assured her. Ralph's compositions came in the second half of the concert. Susanna found herself hoping that Judy would fall asleep again before then, but she remained wide awake.

Ralph's style had changed over the years, but his work continued to be outstanding. Susanna listened, enthralled.

"Goodness, and to think I've met Ralph Ewart-James in the flesh, even if it was only for a few moments. He is talented, isn't he, Susie? I do like his music," Judy enthused.

They became so engrossed that they did

not hear Tom until he opened the bedroom door. "Hallo, you two."

"Hallo, darling," Judy greeted him. "We're listening to Ralph Ewart-James' concert."

"Yes, I've been listening in the car." He perched on the edge of the bed. "Must be nearly finished now. You've made a marvellous job of tidying up downstairs, Susie. I hardly recognise the place—and she's done the ironing, Judy. She's missing her vocation; she'd obviously make a superb mother's help."

"I know," Judy said. "She's an angel —now shush and let's hear the end of this concert."

Susanna felt herself growing tense as she realised that any moment now the orchestra would play *Susanna's Song*. She swallowed hard; perhaps they wouldn't play it after all. Perhaps Ralph had only been teasing—and then his voice came over the radio.

"And now I should like to end this evening's concert with a piece of music that I have dedicated to a very dear friend of mine, the accomplished pianist and composer Susanna Rosenfield, who I believe is listening tonight. It's called, *Susanna's Song.*"

The colour suffused Susanna's cheeks. This was Ralph's music—his especial message to her. The orchestral arrangement was so very beautiful that it brought a lump to her throat. She did not raise her eyes until the music had ended and the applause had died down.

Judy switched off the radio. "That was magificent. Of course, I remember now, didn't Ralph Ewart-James have an affair with Susanna Rosenfield? And his wife turned up and created a scene in some Italian hotel. Susanna Rosenfield left the concert tour almost overnight and virtually nothing has been heard of her since. I seem to remember there was quite a bit about it in the papers at the time . . ." She trailed off abruptly. "Oh, dear, am I being indiscreet? I just wondered if he was going to marry her now that he's divorced."

Susanna desperately wished that she

could escape from the room. She clutched the sides of her chair as if for support, aware that Tom was studying her curiously. With a supreme effort she got to her feet and said, in what she hoped was a normal tone, "Ah, now that is the sixty-thousand-dollar question. Judy, it's high time you were asleep—would you like some hot milk?"

Downstairs Tom said hesitantly, "You don't have to answer me if you don't want to, Susie, but is there any possibility that you are Susanna Rosenfield?"

She looked at him helplessly and passed a hand wearily across her forehead. "I thought you'd guess eventually. I take it Judy doesn't suspect?"

He shook his head. "No, and I certainly shan't tell her—not without your permission—you must forgive her for chattering on so just now. I've been putting two and two together over the past few days and then tonight I only had to watch your face when the orchestra was playing *Susanna's Song*, and then to see your reaction to Judy's words just now,

242

to know that I was right—I'm sorry, Susie, for blowing your cover."

She smiled at that. "That's all right—Mark knows anyway. It was foolish of me really trying to keep quiet, especially when you, Tom, should have been the very person that I confided in."

Susanna took Judy her supper drink and stayed to chat for a few moments. Then, over coffee, she told Tom a very brief outline of what had happened in Italy. He nodded, not interrupting, and when she had finished he stroked his chin and said, "Well, that's all water under the bridge. All I know is that I'm honoured to have you as our organist, Susie. Do you think you'll resume your former career some day?"

Susanna sighed. "Tom, I really don't know. Part of me wants to, but I've been happy here in Bridgethorpe and I'm not sure that I want to revert to my old life-style. It wasn't all a bed of roses, as you can imagine."

"You can give of yourself in different ways, you know," Tom said reflectively.

"You could continue to use your gift for music to help youngsters like Timothy Carstairs. Judy, the children and myself have grown very fond of you, and I know Judy would be devastated if you went away. Remember that you're probably needed here in Bridgethorpe equally as much as on any platform. And, if things get tough come to us, we'll always be here ready to help you."

"Bless you, Tom," she said huskily, "I will remember that." And she realised she was glad that he knew the truth at last.

8

GRAHAM Bryant asked Susanna to call to see him before she left Ravenscourt College on Thursday evening. She felt a bit apprehensive, wondering what he wanted.

"I heard from George Purbright this morning, Miss Price," he informed her. "He doesn't reckon to return much before the end of term and certainly not in time to take over the musical presentation for Speech Day. How's it coming along, by the way?"

Susanna told him and then added, "I think I shall need some extra time for rehearsals after half-term."

"Oh, I feel sure something can be arranged. I'm most impressed with the work you and Mark Liston are doing. George Purbright is a fine music teacher, but he is inclined to be a little on the conventional side. I was passing the music room the other day, and I was so interested in what I heard that I just had to stop and listen. My dear Miss Price, you really are most accomplished. I had no idea you had such a nice singing voice."

Susanna smiled. "I must admit I'm enjoying taking the classes."

The Head cleared his throat. "Now Cynthia and I would like you to come to dinner one evening soon. It must be a bit lonely for you over in that cottage with your father away. Are you free this Saturday?"

"Why, yes, I'd enjoy that very much—thank you." Susanna felt it was an invitation she could hardly have refused and, besides, Mark would no doubt be asked as well. She hadn't seen much of him during the past week; it was almost as if he had been avoiding her.

Graham Bryant beamed. "That's splendid. We'll say seven for seven thirty, shall we? And I'll come and fetch you. I'm afraid it'll be a bit quiet—just Cynthia and I and probably Mr.

Kingsman. Some friends of Amanda's have hired a boat on the Broads and she and Mark Liston are joining them for the day."

Graham Bryant could have absolutely no idea of the impact his words had on Susanna. She felt thoroughly depressed as she cycled back to Lavender Cottage for Mark hadn't mentioned anything to her about this trip on the Broads. How could she have been so foolish as to have ever supposed that he cared for her when it was painfully obvious that he was becoming increasingly interested in Mandy?

Mrs. Gotobed was looking out of her cottage window. She beckoned urgently to Susanna who indicated the bicycle and wheeled it into the garden before going to find out what was the matter. By that time, Mrs. Gotobed had come to the front door with a bouquet of glorious deep-red roses in her arms.

"These came for you, dear—Interflora —aren't they a picture? I reckoned they must be from that gentleman in the Rolls.''

Susanna thanked Mrs. Gotobed profusely, refused her offer of a cup of tea and, to the old lady's great disappointment, did not even look at the card.

Once inside Lavender Cottage Susanna opened the envelope. The message read: ''For Susie, all my love, Ralph.'' Knowing Mrs. Gotobed she had probably taken it upon herself to have a peep. Susanna smiled and, humming softly, went to fill some vases. Red roses for love. Ralph had always had a romantic streak in his nature. In the past he had sent her roses whenever the concerts had gone well.

Susanna supposed it would be halfway round the village by the following day that her admirer in the Rolls had sent her red roses. She was gently amused. There was no way in which she could get Ralph to understand that she would prefer a more simple gift and that he couldn't bribe her into playing in the concert. She arranged the delicate blooms carefully.

They lit the sitting-room with a fiery glow —like rubies—and their heady perfume pervaded the air.

On an impulse Susanna extracted a few of the blooms and took them across to Mrs. Gotobed who was now in her garden. The old lady's face lit up with pleasure. "Why, Miss Price, it's years since anyone gave me roses—that is a kind thought. It really is."

"Well there were far too many for me and I thought you might like them."

Ralph never did things by halves, she reflected in amusement.

"Came from London, didn't he—so someone told me," Mrs. Gotobed said, obviously convinced that it had been Ralph who had sent the bouquet. Susanna agreed that he did. As she returned to her cottage she caught sight of the polyanthus which she had long since planted in the border and which had finished flowering for the time being—like her relationship with Mark, and she smiled wryly. It would have been different if he had only told her what he really felt for her. He must never know that she had believed him to be serious about their relationship and that she had allowed herself to fall a little in love with him.

Judy was very much better by Friday, but feeling rather low and unlike her usual cheery self. "What you need," Susanna told her briskly, "is a nice walk in the fresh air. It'll do you a power of good and it's a beautiful day."

They set out from the rectory and, turning down a lane past the church, crossed a stile and walked along a footpath by the side of a field.

"They've planted sugar beet in here," Susanna informed her, "and all along this hedgerow in the autumn are blackberries."

Judy coughed. "Yes, it's very lovely round here. Tom has always wanted a country living and we thought it would be good for the children. I do like being in Bridgethorpe, but just now and then I get a pang of nostalgia for city life."

"I know how you feel," Susanna

sympathised. "The countryside takes a bit of getting used to, I'll agree. I'd always lived in a city or town before coming here and I wondered how I'd adapt. In the beginning I was like a fish out of water, but gradually the slower pace and tranquillity of it all took a hold on me and now I love it here . . ." She trailed off, suddenly aware of the enormity of what she was contemplating—throwing away all this to resume her career.

Judy looked at her keenly. "You know you're very different from how I imagined when I first met you. I thought you were timid and mouse-like, but you're not a bit like that really, and I suspect that you haven't always led such a quiet life. You don't seem to have any past. I know I'm being curious, Susie."

Susanna picked a dog-rose from the hedgerow. "Oh, that's all right. You see, up until recently I haven't been able to talk about what happened previous to my coming here, because I found it all rather painful, but now I can face up to it more easily and one day soon I'll tell you, although it's nothing very remarkable. I came to Bridgethorpe because I needed to be somewhere quiet for a while to sort myself out. During these past months you've helped me to come out of my shell, Judy." She smiled as she uttered the words, remembering the day at Brancaster with Mark. "The trouble is, just recently I've become a bit restless and I've been wondering if I ought to contemplate moving on before I get into a rut. You see I'm approaching my thirtieth birthday and it seems a sort of milestone."

Judy laughed. "You wait until you're nearly forty like me, lovey! Well I hope you're not going to suddenly decide to leave Bridgethorpe just when we've become friends. I should miss you dreadfully. So when is your birthday?" Susanna told her rather reluctantly. "Well, we must do something to celebrate. Oh, look there on the fence! Someone's been catching moles. I do so hate it when they string them up like that."

"Poor things—shall we turn back now? You must be getting tired."

"Yes, I do still feel a bit weak." Judy blew her nose. "I'd better call in the shop for some more tissues on the way back. I must buck up because it's half-term at the end of next week and we've arranged to have Timothy Carstairs to stay—did Tom tell you?"

"No, actually he didn't. That is kind of you, Judy."

They discussed the boy for a few moments. "Graham said Tim's grandparents seemed quite relieved, apparently," Judy told her. "Poor kid. It's a good job Graham's such a caring Head. At least the boy's got some security at school."

"Yes, Graham Bryant is a very nice person. As a matter of fact, he and Cynthia have asked me to dinner tomorrow night. I can't imagine what we'll find to talk about."

"Won't Mark be there?" Judy asked.

Susanna tried to sound casual. "No, apparently not. He and Mandy are joining some friends of hers on the Broads for the day."

Judy shot her a knowing glance. "I'm sorry, Susie, have I put my foot in it? I thought things were working out OK between you and Mark."

Susanna stooped to pick up a fir cone. "I think I read too much into the relationship. Anyway, it's best not to become too involved. I've decided that it usually only leads to heartache in the end." She was unable to keep a tinge of bitterness from her voice.

"You sound as if you're speaking from bitter experience," Judy remarked.

"Well, perhaps I am. I'm afraid I never have been much good when it comes to affairs of the heart. They usually seem to turn sour on me. Anyway, Mandy's far more vivacious than I am. She plays tennis and badminton and is the life and soul of the party whilst I just play the piano!"

Judy took her arm gently. "So that's what's making you restless is it? Well, I'm sure everything will sort itself out—given time."

Susanna smiled as she remembered the red roses that filled her sitting-room with their sweet fragrance. Oh, yes, everything would sort itself out, but not quite in the way that Judy meant.

Ralph rang up at just turned six o'clock that evening. "I've been rehearsing all afternoon and I haven't had a moment. Did you manage to hear Wednesday's concert?"

"Yes, it was superb—and I got your roses yesterday. Thank you, Ralph, they're gorgeous. I was very moved by *Susanna's Song*."

"Moved enough to come and play for us, eh?"

She took a deep breath, knowing that once she had committed herself there would be no going back on her word. "Yes, Ralph, I'll play in that concert."

"That's my girl—I knew I could rely on you. You'll be magnificent so never fear. I'll help you through, my darling."

"Well, you'd better fill me in on the details if you're going abroad again, Ralph."

"Oh, there's no hurry. I'll give you a ring from Paris sometime."

"But, I shall need to know what to play so that I can start practising," Susanna persisted.

"That goes without saying—the second Rachmaninov concerto, of course, what else?"

Susanna felt herself grow cold. "No, Ralph, I won't play that. It's wrong of you to ask me. It has far too many memories associated with it."

"Then that's all the more reason why you should play it, to exorcise the ghosts." Susanna argued the toss with him for several moments and then finally capitulated. "Good, I'm glad you've seen reason, Susie," he said triumphantly.

They discussed the details of the concert for a few moments and then suddenly remembering something she said: "Ralph, I ought to have asked you this before—what exactly is this concert in aid of?"

"Oh, some special equipment for the local hospital primarily," he explained. "Now, I intend to be in England for your birthday, Susie. This year I'm going to make sure it's a very special birthday indeed, to make up for those I've missed."

She felt a warm glow inside her. "I'll look forward to that. Now you'd better go or you won't be ready for tonight's concert. I shall be listening."

"I should hope so indeed. I suppose you saw the write-up in the papers?"

"Yes," she replied briefly. The reviews of Wednesday's concert had been good and the gossip columnists had asked: "Are we to gather that Susanna Rosenfield is here in England and can we assume that she and Ralph Ewart-James are now back together again?"

He laughed. "You wait until they get wind of the concert. Well, goodbye, my darling—for now."

Susanna replaced the receiver and sat

as if in a trance. The whole pattern of her life was about to change once again. Now that she had actually told Ralph of her decision she felt extremely apprehensive. Supposing she could not play so well as in the past? Was she really up to concert standard nowadays? She had no one to advise her—just her own judgement to rely upon and only two rehearsals before the performance. It was nearly two and a half years since she had last played with an orchestra. Her stomach turned over at the enormity of the task before her.

Susanna took her supper into the sitting-room. There was just time to listen to her own recording of the Rachmaninov concerto before Ralph's concert. She always found it a strange experience listening to herself playing. She realised that over the years she had not lost her technique, just her sparkle. She had once told Timothy Carstairs that music should come from the soul, and knew that if only she could play with her very being then everything would be all right. She would practise every spare moment between now and the concert. She was suddenly determined that she would give a brilliant performance just to prove that she was still capable of it. She would do it for her father's sake. He would be overjoyed when he learned of her decision. Yes, she would do it for him.

As the train sped towards Yorkshire on Thursday morning, Susanna found that she had plenty of opportunity to think about what had been happening recently. Mark had briefly told her that he was staying with his family in Southwold for part of his half-term holiday and then going on to visit friends in London. He had not suggested that he and Susanna should spend any time together. She still found it hard to accept that their romance had been so shortlived and that she no longer had a part in his plans.

During dinner at the Bryants, Cynthia had let slide a remark which had stung Susanna. "Mark Liston is such a delightful person. Mandy is very fond of him—they have so much in common. We had thought she might find it rather dull here, but now that she's met Mark we rather think there might be a romance in the air."

It was evident that Susanna had been a fool to have imagined that Mark had ever been serious about her. Her cheeks burned as she remembered his kisses, for she realised that because of her affair with Ralph he had probably thought she was a soft option, only too ready for a flirtation. Well, she was just glad that she had had her eyes opened in time before she had made a complete idiot of herself for the second time running.

At least she was more mature now, able to think out situations without being so impetuous and getting into such a state. Now that Ralph had found her again perhaps things would work out all right between them after all.

She had lain awake several nights thinking about the concert and wondering if she had really made the right decision. She realised that, as her father had said, it could prove to be the turning-point of her life, the deciding factor as to whether she remained in Bridgethorpe or resumed her musical career. Everything hinged on that concert and the way in which she was received by the public. There was absolutely no way in which she could back down now either, for there had been a piece in the paper announcing that she was taking part. Tom had pointed it out to her discreetly in the staffroom with a quiet aside of congratulations.

Her father met her at the station. His verdict as he took a look at her pale face and noted the dark shadows under her eyes was: "You're looking tired and pale, Susie, and I'll guarantee it's because you're worrying about that concert."

Later, as they took a stroll through the village after supper she said, "Of course, you're right, Dad. You know me so well. I think perhaps I've bitten off more than I can chew. It's the concert one week and the Ravenscourt musical presentation the next. Oh, I just don't know whether I'm up to it any more. Everyone is going to expect so much of me."

"You'll be all right, Susie," her father assured her. "It's a marvellous opportunity and Ralph Ewart-James is doing the right thing in helping you back on the road to success again. I don't know why you're so anxious. After all, you know the Rachmaninov backwards, don't you?"

She laughed, "Practically. Ralph wants me to play some of my own compositions too in the second half—the unpublished ones."

"Your Bridgethorpe medley, as I call them? Well they're good; they should be heard. So what's troubling you really, Susie? Just nerves?"

They stopped by the pond to watch the geese. She couldn't find the words to tell him about Mark Liston, and so she merely said, "There's a distinct possibility that the concert will be broadcast and I'm just not sure that I can face up to all the publicity. Supposing it's a flop."

"Darling, it won't be. Look, Susie, do this concert for me and for the hospital. Don't worry about anyone else. If, at the end of it, you decide that you want to pick up the threads from where you left off and resume your career, then I'll be over the moon. If not, well I'll understand—either way, I want what's best for you." He took her arm. "So what about Ralph? Are you still in love with him?"

She sighed. "Oh, I'm just not sure any more. I've told him not to rush me. I've got to get used to the idea that he's come back into my life again. After what happened my faith in him was severely shaken, as you know."

"What does Catherine have to say about it all?" Robert Price enquired.

"Actually, I haven't told her yet, although she's bound to have seen the newspapers," Susanna said thinking of her practically minded, no-nonsense sister who would not hesitate to speak her mind. She would, no doubt, tell Susanna that she considered her to be a prize idiot to have allowed Ralph anywhere near her again after the way he had treated her in the past.

Robert Price looked at Susanna

astutely. He was convinced that something else was troubling his daughter, but he resolved not to question her any further, feeling certain that she would tell him about it all in her own good time.

The few days' change of scenery did Susanna a world of good. Aunt Jessie fussed over her like a mother hen. On the Sunday Robert Price drove his daughter to the dales. The air was bracing and Susanna felt invigorated. Bridgethorpe and her problems seemed very far away.

After their picnic lunch she leant back and, closing her eyes, soaked up the glorious June sunshine. She suddenly found herself wondering what Mark was doing. Annoyed with herself she struggled into a sitting position. Why did he always have to get in the way and spoil things just as she was beginning to get matters sorted out in her mind? There had been times just lately when she had found herself wishing that she had never set eyes on Mark Liston. He had upset the orderly pattern of her life in Bridgethorpe. If it hadn't been for Mark she would have found it far simpler to have made a decision about her future now, but he had caused her to have an element of doubt that had developed into a cloud to obliterate her otherwise crystal-clear reasoning.

"Susie, you're miles away—what are you dreaming about?" her father asked her.

Susanna forced a smile. "Nothing important. It's just nice to relax."

Robert Price poured out some more coffee. "Do have a garibaldi biscuit. Your aunt ordered countless packets for the shop and no one seems to like them except for us so we have to keep on eating them—you'd better take some back with you."

Susanna laughed. "James Davidson calls them 'squashed fly biscuits'!"

Her father chuckled. "Very apt—you know you're looking better already, Susie. You'll soon be ready to face the entire world if necessary. You'll come through, you'll see. You always have done in the past. Remember, when you play in that concert you're going to give pleasure to a lot of people including myself."

Susanna shredded a blade of grass. The sun shone down from a hyacinth-blue sky. Her problems had drifted away like the clouds. "I'll do my very best," she promised.

"It's not going to do," Susanna told the choir sternly. "A half-term holiday and you've forgotten everything we've ever taught you. Do you realise just how little time we've got before Speech Day? Now we'll take it from the beginning again. Mr. Liston, do you have any suggestions?"

Mark standing at the side of the room spread his hands in a gesture of despair. "Well, we could of course scrap the whole idea. I've never heard such a pathetic noise in all my life. I'll tell you what, Miss Price, shall we show them how it could be done?"

Susanna quickly caught on. "Yes, why not indeed—sit down and listen!"

Mark had an extremely powerful voice

which blended well with Susanna's clear soprano. She had taken singing lessons for about three years and could make a fair performance. The boys listened attentively as their teachers demonstrated the particular song, and then applauded energetically.

"Right!" Mark said. "Let's begin again, shall we? Stop being so apathetic and put some life into it."

The singing was considerably improved this time, but nowhere near the standard Susanna had hoped for. After the boys had been dismissed, Mark said, "Dare I enquire how the *Daniel Jazz* is coming along?"

"Oh, now that is a little better than this, I'll grant you." She tried to make light of it. "We'll just have to do the presentation ourselves!"

"Could come to that—the way things are going," he said caustically. "And you will be gratified to learn that old George intends to attend Speech Day."

Susanna sighed. "Yes, I know. Mr. Bryant told me, and he'll no doubt have forty fits. I'm fully aware that what we're doing isn't at all George Purbright's idea of what one should put on for the parents."

Mark frowned. "Of course, you do realise that your London concert takes place just a week before this affair?"

Susanna returned his gaze without flickering an eyelid and said coolly, "You have no need to worry, Mark. Mr. Bryant is going to allow me extra time for rehearsals and so I can always cancel my private piano lessons for one week, if necessary, to enable me to have some afternoon rehearsals here, and I can come in on the Friday too. It will be all right, you'll see."

"Well, I just wish I could share your optimism," he told her rather coldly, and her heart sank at his words.

Susanna encountered Cynthia Bryant in the entrance hall. "Ah, there you are, Miss Price. The rector is still talking with my husband at the present moment. He said he'd arranged to give you a lift home, and so I told him I'd give you a cup of tea whilst you're waiting."

They walked over to the house and Cynthia Bryant ushered Susanna into the sitting-room and then went off to make the tea. Amanda looked up with a smile. "Oh, hallo, Susanna, isn't Mark with you?"

"No, he's got some work to do before supervising prep."

"Oh, a pity." Amanda indicated her knitting. "I'm making him a sweater and I needed to measure him. It's one of those chunky ones so it shouldn't take too long."

"Yes, it's a nice colour," Susanna said flatly, realising that anything that might have once been between her and Mark was now totally over, for Amanda Bryant was obviously his new girlfriend.

"Yes, well it's a sort of thank-you to him for taking me to London. We had a marvellous time."

Susanna swallowed hard. "You—you went to London with Mark over half-term?"

Amanda studied her knitting pattern, screwing up her face anxiously.

"Oh, I do hope I've done this right. I've not attempted anything quite so ambitious before. Yes, just for Monday and Tuesday. Do you know anything about knitting patterns, Susanna?"

"No, I'm afraid I'm not much good at knitting." She tried hard to conceal her feelings, but found it hard for she realised that she minded about what Mandy had just told her more than she had thought possible.

Cynthia Bryant bustled in with a tea-trolley. "Having a good natter? Surely you're not in trouble with that knitting again, Mandy?" She sighed. "You'd best let me look. Here's your tea, Miss Price —sugar?"

"No, thank you, Mrs. Bryant." Susanna was glad of the tea for it helped to restore her calm. Cynthia Bryant cut some Madeira cake and handed it round.

"Did you have a nice half-term, Miss Price? You went to Yorkshire, didn't you? We missed you playing in church.

Everyone says what a treat it is to hear you."

Susanna smiled, but her heart was heavy. She forced herself to tell Cynthia about Yorkshire, but, all the time, she was thinking about Mark and Mandy and the fact that Mark hadn't mentioned anything to her about their trip to London.

"Wasn't it nice of Mark to take Mandy down to London?" Cynthia said brightly. "She did enjoy herself, didn't you, dear?"

Amanda smiled, looking like the cat that has just got the cream. She was an undeniably pretty little thing with her dark curls and delicate features, and she certainly knew how to win round the men.

Susanna was never more relieved than when Graham Bryant put his head round the door and announced that Tom was ready to drive her home.

"Tim enjoyed himself over half-term," Tom remarked during the short drive to Lavender Cottage.

"Oh, good, I'm glad it worked out," she said rather absently.

"Mm—we liked having him too. He's certainly got a gift for music. Our old piano wondered what had happened to. it. So how's life treating you, Susie? Have you started practising for your London concert yet?"

"Yes, I only hope I haven't made a mistake in agreeing to do it. Mark seems to feel that the Speech Day presentation at Ravenscourt will suffer because my mind's on other matters."

"Nonsense, you'll manage both remarkably well, I'm sure. Will you break the news to Judy or shall I? You do intend to tell her and the Bryants beforehand, don't you?"

Susanna sighed. "I suppose I don't have much option. There's bound to be a write-up in the papers, however small, and something will no doubt be said about my living in Norfolk, so I'd best put them in the picture."

"Well, I must admit one doesn't expect to have famous people cooking their children's supper for them and nursing their wife's cold."

Susanna had to laugh. "Oh, Tom, you are a tonic. I was feeling quite low, what with a lousy rehearsal and one or two other things, and you've made me feel ten times better already."

"Good—that's part of my job. Here we are then, home at last. There's the faithful Tabitha waiting for you at the gate. 'Bye, Susie—everything will be OK, you'll see."

But would it, she asked herself. Her doubts had returned. If only Mark had been there to support her. It hurt her to realise that those kisses had meant nothing to him and she knew that she cared about him more than she was prepared to admit.

Two evenings later Susanna was just about to step into the bath when the phone rang. Hurriedly donning a towelling robe, she raced down the stairs and into her father's study.

"Hello, sweetie," drawled Ralph's voice at the other end of the line, "So what kept you?" He laughed when she told him. "Bet you look ravishing, a pity I'm not there to see you," and her cheeks burned. "Now listen carefully, my darling, because I've only got a very few minutes. I'm booked on a late night flight to England next Thursday. The friend of mine who's been garaging the Rolls is going to meet me at the airport on Friday. I've got a couple of things to attend to in London in the morning so I'll be with you by early afternoon. Now, can you arrange for me to hear the Carstairs boy at around three o'clock?"

"Yes, I should think so. I'll fix it up with Graham Bryant," she told him.

"Good. Susie, we're going to the Maltings at Snape for your birthday treat on Friday night. I didn't tell you before in case I had to disappoint you, sweetie, but it's all arranged."

"Ralph, that's marvellous, but my birthday's not until the Saturday."

"I know that, darling, but it's the best I could do because I've got a rehearsal on the Saturday afternoon for a major concert in the evening. I'm afraid it will literally be a flying visit as I shall have to leave again straight after breakfast on Saturday."

"So how on earth have you managed to get away from the tour?" she asked.

"By allowing a very promising young man his first chance at conducting on Friday night. He'll take the rehearsal on Saturday morning too. Now, tell me—how's the Rachmaninov progressing?"

"Oh, I'm feeling much happier about it," she assured him.

"Good, I knew you would. It'll be quite splendid on the night, you'll see. I've got every confidence in you, Susie. I must go now, darling." He blew a kiss down the phone.

It was not until after Susanna had replaced the receiver that she realised that there were a hundred and one questions she should have asked him. She poured some more hot water into her cooling bath. For a start he had said nothing about accommodation. He obviously thought she would agree to him staying at the cottage on this occasion, but with Mrs. Gotobed for a next-door neighbour, it would be circulated all round the village by the end of the weekend. Besides she knew exactly what Ralph would have in mind, and she felt that she couldn't cope with any further emotional entanglements at present. No, she would ring the pub at Trissingham where he had stayed before and make a reservation for him there. She was aware that he wouldn't like the arrangement, as he had complained that the place was too spartan. Susanna felt delighted at the prospect of going to the Maltings again. She smiled softly; dear Ralph, he knew exactly how to please her.

"Annabel played so well today that I've promised she can see that evening gown of mine before she goes home," Susanna told Judy when she popped in for a cup of tea after her daughter's piano lesson.

"Goodness, I'd forgotten all about that," Judy said, "but it's obvious Annabel hasn't."

Susanna slipped upstairs to fetch the

dress whilst Judy was drinking her tea. It had occurred to Susanna that this would be a golden opportunity to explain things to her friend.

"Oh, it's gorgeous!" Annabel exclaimed fingering the silky aquamarine-coloured material.

"Hold it against you, Susie, so that we can see the effect," Judy said. "You really ought to have put it on for us. Oh that is lovely! It suits your colouring perfectly. Whereabouts did you say the concert was held?"

"Vienna, actually," Susanna said in a matter-of-fact tone.

Judy looked at her in amazement. "Vienna! Susanna, you're not pulling my leg, are you? Did you really play in Vienna?"

Susanna nodded. "Yes, it was a lovely concert. I used to have a much prettier dress than this one, Annabel—at least I thought so. I've a photograph of me wearing that too—would you like to see it?"

"Oh, yes, please, Miss Price. Did you wear that one for a concert as well?"

"Yes, as a matter of fact I did." Judy was looking at Susanna, as if for the first time, a puzzled expression on her face. Susanna went over to her record cases. "I think it's in this one—ah yes, here we are. I wore this dress when I was in Rome."

She handed her recording of the Rachmaninov concerto to Annabel who gazed at the sleeve wide-eyed. "Is that really you, Miss Price? Oh you do look lovely. It doesn't say your name on the top though it says—Susanna Rose—Rose . . ."

Judy looked over her daughter's shoulder, incredulously, "Susanna Rosenfield! Susie, can that really be you?"

"Yes, I am Susanna Rosenfield. At least, that's what I'm called professionally. Rosenfield was my mother's maiden name, actually."

"Are you famous?" Annabel asked in wonder.

Susanna smiled at her young pupil. "At

one time I was, maybe, but not any more. Annabel, would you mind going into the garden for a few minutes? I need to talk to your mother."

Annabel looked disappointed, but went obediently. Judy had lapsed into a stunned silence. Susanna poured more tea for them both.

"I'm sorry, Judy. I didn't intend to spring this on you like this, but you see I just couldn't bring myself to tell you before."

"Whyever not—I'm thrilled. It's just that it'll take a bit of time to get used to the idea. Oh, Susie, what a fool you must think me—and I put my foot in it going on about you and Ralph the other week, didn't I? It's a wonder you're still speaking to me. I must be dreadfully thick-skinned not to have realised the truth before."

"Judy, do try to understand that I didn't intend to deceive you. It's just that I wanted you to accept me as myself. I might never have told you now if Ralph hadn't suddenly turned up out of the blue like that. You see everything's happened rather quickly. Ralph's persuaded me to play in a charity concert in London next weekend—my first for almost two and a half years."

Judy still looked dazed. "I see, so does that mean you're planning to resume your career?"

"Ask me that question again after next Saturday's concert, Judy," Susanna told her gently.

"Well, I suppose I should say I'm very happy for you, but I'm going to miss you dreadfully if you move away. Does Mark know who you really are?"

"Yes, we met once in Vienna. He was doing his journalist stint then. He recognised me soon after he arrived in Bridgethorpe—and, Judy, I'm afraid Tom knows as well. He put two and two together a little while ago."

Judy looked hurt. "And he didn't say anything to me. Whyever not?"

Susanna suddenly felt rather unkind. "I'm sorry, Judy, I asked him not to. I was so afraid that it might alter our friendship when you found out that I put off telling you for as long as I could. You see, I guess I like being ordinary and above all being accepted for myself. You, Tom and Mark have all helped me to become part of society again. I was fast becoming a recluse when you rescued me! Some day I'll tell you what happened to make me come to Bridgethorpe in the first place. I promise I'll try to explain things to you."

Judy pushed back her hair. "Oh, what a fool I've been thinking you were interested in Mark when all the time there's Ralph Ewart-James!"

Susanna wasn't quite sure how to reply to this. "He's only recently come back into my life again, believe you me. Things just didn't work out between Mark and myself. He seems to prefer Mandy's company." She replaced her record in the case. "Actually, Ralph's arranged to hear Timothy Carstairs play on Friday afternoon."

Judy looked surprised. "But I thought

Mr. Ewart-James was in Paris at the present moment."

Susanna laughed. "Yes, so he is, but he's coming over especially to take me to the Maltings on Friday evening—that's Ralph for you! He'll have to leave again early on Saturday, in order to be back in Paris for a rehearsal in the afternoon."

Judy smiled. "Well, have a lovely time, Susie. What a pity he can't stay on for your birthday."

A knock sounded at the front door. "Oh dear, that must be Mrs. Jenkins already. Could you possibly let her in, Judy, whilst I take this dress upstairs?"

Ralph was late on Friday. It was practically two thirty when he eventually arrived looking drawn and tired.

"I've had a filthy journey," he said sweeping Susanna into his arms.

"I'd better ring Graham Bryant to let him know we'll be late and then I'm going to get you something to eat," Susanna told him.

Ralph sank into an armchair and indicated his duty-free carrier-bag.

"I need a drink, Susie, middle of the afternoon or not—find me a glass would you, my darling?"

She fetched him one, recognising how strung up he was, and then went to phone the Head.

When Ralph was rested they drove to Ravenscourt where Cynthia Bryant was anxiously waiting to greet them. Timothy seemed nervous, but Susanna spoke reassuringly to him and tactfully managed to dissuade Cynthia from staying to listen.

Timothy made a hash of the first few bars of the Chopin he had chosen to play and Ralph barked, "Begin again!" Susanna could tell from the boy's face how tense he was feeling, and realised how much it all meant to him. "You're trying too hard, Tim," she whispered. "Relax—take a deep breath and play for me," and she smiled at him encouragingly.

To her great relief, her words seemed to do the trick for the boy began to play with greater confidence. Glancing over at Ralph she saw that he was listening intently. He made Timothy play several pieces for him and then, beckoning him over, shook him by the hand.

"Well done, young man. You've got talent and should have no trouble in embarking on a musical career. Now, you must listen to everything Miss-er-Price tells you. You couldn't have a finer teacher. I'll see what I can do for you."

The boy's face shone. "Thank you, sir," he breathed. "Thank you very much."

"That was splendid, Tim," Susanna congratulated him and he returned to his lessons happy in the knowledge that he had done well.

"The boy's undeniably good," Ralph told the Bryants without preamble. "Of course, he needs far more lessons. Susanna can take him a long way, but he's lacking the experience of playing in public and needs competition. I shall need to speak with his father."

"That could prove difficult," Graham

Bryant explained. 'He's in the Middle East!"

Ralph rubbed his chin. "Then I'll have to contact him because we need to sort something out fairly quickly. In the mean time, he must have more lessons and more practising time—an hour a day is as good as useless. I'll see what can be arranged about him making his début as a young musician—I think we shall be seeing a lot of this young man in the future."

Cynthia beamed. "How very exciting. We can't thank you enough for coming here."

They talked for a few moments longer and then Ralph consulted his watch and said apologetically, "I'm afraid you'll have to excuse us now. Susanna and I are going to the Maltings at Snape for a concert this evening."

"How lovely," Cynthia said, trying to hide her disappointment that he was leaving so soon. "We had hoped we could persuade you to play for us, Mr. Ewart

James. My husband and I so enjoyed listening to your concert the other evening."

Ralph pretended to look puzzled. "Now why on earth should you want to hear me play when you have Susanna? She can play for you a hundred times better than me."

Susanna and Ralph went shortly afterwards, leaving the Bryants looking distinctly mystified.

"That was wicked of you, Ralph—now I shall have to say something!" Susanna chided him, but he only laughed.

"High time too. Anyway, there won't be any need. They'll find out soon enough, and if they can't see what's beneath their very noses . . ."

"Be fair—they've only heard me play church music," she protested.

Susanna dressed carefully for her night out with Ralph. She chose to wear an evening gown in delicate shades of misty blue and green. She brushed her hair until it shone and, catching back the sides with a black velvet bow, left the rest to cascade in soft waves. She discarded the spectacles for her contact lenses and wore rather more make-up than usual.

"That's my Susie," Ralph said approvingly. "You look stunning. Here, I've brought you a little present for your birthday, sweetheart." He handed her a black jewel case. "Sorry there wasn't time to wrap it—I'd like you to open it now."

She pressed the catch and the lid sprang open to reveal a most exquisite pair of diamond earrings, sparkling iridescently on a bed of black velvet.

"Ralph, they're beautiful!" she gasped. "But they're far too expensive."

He laughed. "Nonsense, Susie, I'm a wealthy man and I haven't given you anything for several Christmases and birthdays now. Come here and let me put them in for you, my darling." His fingers moved gently over her ear-lobes. "There —quite perfect. I'll put these you were wearing in the box."

He held her to him caressing her tenderly. "You are so lovely! If only you'd wear my ring tonight you'd make me a very happy man indeed. Oh, Susie,

I need you. I want you to be with me all the time. Will you marry me, my darling —soon?"

He had taken her unawares and she was unable to meet his eyes, afraid that he might see how uncertain she was. She did not want to spoil the evening so she murmured, "Just give me a little more time, Ralph."

"All right," he said softly, "I'll wait for your answer until after next Saturday's concert," and his lips came fiercely down on hers.

9

SUSANNA and Ralph dined at the Maltings' restaurant with its scenic view overlooking the estuary and marshes. Although Susanna had been to the Aldeburgh Music Festival on several occasions before, the atmosphere of the Maltings never failed to fill her with a sense of excitement. Here in a tranquil setting throbbed the very heart of the musical world. It was in a converted windmill nearby that Benjamin Britten had composed his most brilliant works.

The auditorium itself was pleasingly simplistic with roof trusses made from Douglas fir, natural red-brick walls and ash-framed cane chairs.

"Apparently they got the notion of having these cane chairs from the Wagner opera-house at Bayreuth," Ralph informed Susanna, settling himself more comfortably. Susanna studied her programme.

"The architects certainly knew what they were doing when they created this concert hall," she said admiringly.

The concert met up to Susanna's expectations in every way. She sat enraptured drifting away on Mozart's piano concerto No. 9 in E flat major. As the pianist began to play the Andantino, Susanna found herself longing to be a part of it all once again.

During the interval Ralph took her arm as they strolled along the banks of the Alde. "Enjoying it?" he asked her.

"Tremendously, thank you, Ralph. I love this place."

"Hmm it's got a certain magical quality all of its own, I'll agree."

They paused to look across the river at the saltings and the Iken cliff. The sky was a vast expanse of misty-blue; the silence broken only by the gentle river noises. "This is certainly an incomparable setting for a concert hall and the acoustics in that auditorium are quite remarkable.

Tell me, Susie, are you in the right frame of mind now for our concert?"

She smiled. "Yes, and growing more so as the evening progresses. This is just the sort of stimulus I needed."

"One day I should like to conduct a concert here," Ralph mused. "I sometimes think I've been abroad so long that they've forgotten all about me." But his words were proved to be wrong just a few moments later for, as they re-entered the foyer, a flash bulb went off. His pressure on her elbow increased and his mouth set in a grim line. "Those wretched reporters are everywhere—someone's recognised us!"

Susanna suddenly realised that she no longer minded and when inevitably the press appeared and fired a barrage of questions at her she managed to deal with the situation calmly.

When the concert was over Ralph was in a strangely subdued mood. Susanna however, was on cloud nine. The music had filled her with ecstasy and inspiration and she ached to play the piano. She knew that she was now ready to face her public again.

It was very late when they reached Bridgethorpe. Ralph drove the Rolls round to the garage at the back of Lavender Cottage to avoid disturbing Mrs. Gotobed. When he entered the cottage Susanna noticed how utterly exhausted he was looking and threw her arms about his neck.

"Oh, Ralph, you've made me extremely happy tonight. I've had a truly marvellous time. Thank you!"

He pulled her to him, his grey eyes suddenly alight with passion.

"Then don't send me away, Susie, let me stay here with you tonight. We've got such a little time together." His kiss was passionate, his fingers bruised her bare shoulders, moving slowly down over the thin material of her gown setting her aflame with sudden desire.

Suddenly she jerked away. "I'm making you some coffee and then you must go," she said firmly.

"You're cruel, Susie, tantalisingly

cruel," he told her, "but I love you all the same."

Even though he still had the power to attract her physically, she knew that she was no longer in love with him for she had given her heart to Mark Liston. By the time she returned with the coffee Ralph was fast asleep curled up on the sofa breathing heavily. For the first time she noted the lines etched beneath his eyes and the grey pallor of his cheeks. He had aged in the years since she had left him. She had not got the heart to disturb him. He had given her a wonderful evening and she knew that she would have to grant him his wish and let him stay, even though it wasn't how either of them had anticipated it. After ringing the inn at Trissingham, she crept back into the sitting-room and covered Ralph with a travel rug. He would be stiff and cramped when he woke, but he needed to sleep. Dropping a kiss on his forehead she tiptoed upstairs to bed.

Susanna was awakened the following morning by the sound of Ralph splashing around in the bathroom. Looking at her alarm clock she hurriedly grabbed her négligée and went out on the landing.

"Ralph, you're going to be late—I'll get you some breakfast."

The bathroom door flew open and Ralph emerged dressed in trousers and singlet, a towel draped round his neck. "Good-morning, my darling, a very happy birthday." His hands encircled her waist, pulling her to him.

"You look delectable, my sweet. You know I'm very tempted to catch a later flight. I missed my opportunity last night, didn't I? What a fool I was to have fallen asleep like that!" He covered her with kisses.

"Have you finished with the bathroom?" she demanded rather shakily, and pushing him away went to freshen up. She did not bother dressing for there wasn't time.

She had just gone downstairs when there was a loud rap at the front door. Thinking it was the postman she went to open it. Mark stood on the step; his brown eyes travelled over her and she felt the colour stain her cheeks as she remembered her attire.

"I know it's early, Susie, but I've got some extra coaching to do at nine and I wanted to wish you a happy birthday." He handed her a flat parcel.

Her heart sang. "Well, thank you, Mark, but how on earth did you know?"

He grinned. "A little bird whispered in my ear. I thought if I left it until later on you might be out, as I understand Ralph is in Bridgethorpe."

Susanna pushed back her cloud of silken hair. She did not realise how lovely she looked. Her négligée had come unfastened revealing the peach-soft skin of her throat and shoulders and her softly curving figure in the clinging turquoise nightdress.

"I'm sorry about my appearance—I overslept," she murmured retying her belt more securely.

"Don't be sorry, you look enchanting . . ." He trailed off, his eyes widening. Susanna hardly needed to turn round for she knew what she would see. Ralph was coming down the stairs two at a time, buttoning his shirt cuffs and looking totally unconcerned. He came to stand behind Susanna placing a hand possessively on her shoulder. "Good-morning, Mr. Liston—we meet again. Susie, darling, shall I get the breakfast?"

Susanna was temporarily rendered speechless.

"I'm sorry," Mark said coolly. "I didn't realise you had company. Thoughtless of me—enjoy your birthday, Susanna," and, before she could find her voice, he had gone leaving her standing there clutching his gift.

Susanna was indescribably upset because she knew Ralph had deliberately put in an appearance in order to assert his claim on her over Mark's. How could she expect Mark to believe the truth even if she ever got the chance to explain things to him? Ralph was obviously highly amused by the situation and totally unabashed. She tried not to let him see how much she cared.

Ralph departed shortly afterwards. For Susanna the elation of the previous evening had gone. The post arrived whilst she was upstairs dressing. She opened it without much enthusiasm and then, going into the lounge, picked up Mark's present. She removed the wrapping paper and inside was a framed water-colour print of Blakeney Quay with a card which read: "Have a happy birthday, love Mark." Suddenly the tears came; she could not help herself. She knew now that she was hopelessly in love with Mark and that the situation was totally impossible. Even if she plucked up sufficient courage to tell Mark how she felt about him he would probably never believe her and, in any case, he was now involved with Amanda Bryant. Tabitha came and wound herself round her mistress's legs, sensing that something was wrong.

Susanna was still sitting holding the print when another knock came on the front door. She remained still, hoping whoever it was would go away, but then she heard the back door opening and Judy's voice called out:

"Susie, are you at home?" Susanna desperately looked round for her spectacles but couldn't find them. She ineffectually scrubbed her face on a tissue and reluctantly went into the kitchen.

"Oh, there you are," Judy greeted her. "I found the door open so I let myself in. I know Ralph's gone because I saw the Rolls, so I thought I'd come to wish you a happy birthday . . ." She trailed off suddenly. "Susie, whatever's wrong? You've been crying!"

Susanna sniffed and fumbled for her handkerchief. "Don't mind me, I'm afraid you've just caught me at a bad moment. It's just that—that . . ." The tears coursed down her cheeks and she averted her head struggling for control and sank onto a stool. Judy came and sat beside her.

"You're bound to miss Ralph and to be all keyed up with the concert next week —it's only natural. It's a pity he's had to go tearing back to Paris like that. Did you have a good time last night?"

Susanna nodded blindly and then, covering her face with her hands, began to sob quietly. Judy patted her back gently as if she had been Annabel.

"Mark came here this morning," Susanna blurted out at last and she gave a rather garbled account of what had happened, finishing, "Mark doesn't know how I feel about him and now he never will."

Light suddenly dawned on Judy. "You mean it really is Mark you care about and not Ralph after all?" Susanna nodded. "And I suppose he thinks you're going to marry Ralph?"

"Yes, but it's all quite hopeless anyway because Mark's keen on Amanda Bryant," Susanna said miserably.

"Oh dear, what a mess, Susie!" Judy got to her feet looking perplexed. "Tell you what, shall I make us both a nice cup of tea?"

Susanna went upstairs to bathe her face and when she came down again she felt considerably calmer. "I'm sorry for being such an idiot, Judy."

"Well, if you can't cry in the privacy of your own home where can you?" Judy said briskly. "I do sometimes, I can assure you, and, anyway, I barged in on you. Now get this down you and you'll feel a sight better."

They went into the sitting-room and Judy stood surveying the sofa with its crumpled travel rug. "A pity Mark didn't see this!"

Susanna smiled wryly. "It wouldn't really have proved anything, would it?" She suddenly noticed the half empty whisky bottle and her eyes widened. Judy followed her gaze. "Taken to drinking, has he?"

"More so than normal, I fear. This was full." She opened the window and sighed deeply. "The trouble is I'm beginning to feel sort of guilty where Ralph's concerned. He's been so good to me in the past in spite of everything that's happened. Whatever shall I do?"

Judy frowned. "Well, you've got quite

300

a problem, I'll agree, and I'm not sure quite how to advise you. Look, why don't you forget all about it for the rest of today, eh? Now, how do you feel about joining us for a picnic in Thetford Chase this afternoon? Unless of course, you've got other plans."

"No, actually I haven't—that would be lovely, Judy."

"Right, that's settled then. I've left Annabel at home still making your present. I've just remembered Tom and mine's still in the kitchen. By the way, did you see the papers this morning? I don't want to upset you again, but there was such a lovely photograph of you and Ralph. Here, I brought it with me just in case you hadn't seen it."

Susanna scanned the news cutting briefly. There was the photograph of her and Ralph taken in the foyer at the Maltings and beneath was written:

Seen together again in public last night at The Maltings, Snape, were conductor Ralph Ewart-James and concert pianist Susanna Rosenfield. Rumour has it that Miss Rosenfield has been living in Norfolk since her abrupt departure from a concert tour in Italy two and a half years ago. Miss Rosenfield does not wish to comment on what she has been doing recently, but has confirmed that she will be taking part in the charity concert to be conducted by Ralph Ewart-James in London next Saturday, so perhaps we will learn more then.

"Tom wants to know if you'd like him to make a point of showing this to the Bryants so that they're made aware of the situation," Judy said.

"Oh, yes, please. I must admit that I wasn't quite sure how to tell them." On an impulse Susanna said, "Judy, you've been wonderful to me—a real friend. I'd like to show my appreciation. I've got a couple of spare tickets for the concert. I suppose there's no possibility that you could come?"

Judy's face lit up. "That would be

absolutely marvellous—a real treat. I wonder if I could wangle it. Of course, Tom can't really be spared at such short notice, but if I could perhaps find someone else to accompany me."

A gleam came into Judy's eyes as she took the proffered tickets Susanna produced from the bureau. "I'll certainly do my level best to be there, Susie," she promised.

Susanna caused a few raised eyebrows in church the following morning, for she looked so different from her usual self. She wore an extremely pretty pink and blue Indian cotton dress and had discarded her spectacles. Releasing her hair from its customary knot she had plaited strands from the sides which she had woven round the back of her head, leaving the rest to fall in a ripple of honey-gold waves over her shoulders. Only Judy was aware that Susanna's outward flamboyance disguised her present unhappiness.

Cynthia Bryant seemed to regard Susanna in a new light now that she had learned her true identity. After a few interested questions the Head's wife said, "I do so hope that you will let us hear you play properly some time."

Amused, Susanna replied, "The concert is being broadcast next Saturday and so you could hear me then if you wished—and now, if you'll excuse me, I really must have a word with Mark Liston."

He had reached the lych-gate before she caught up with him. "Mark!" He turned round. "Mark, I wanted to thank you for the print. It's beautiful."

His amber-flecked brown eyes were filled with an unfathomable expression.

"That's OK, I'm glad you liked it."

She realised sadly that they were like strangers again. Amanda Bryant, missing Mark, looked round and called out: "Come on, Mark—we're keeping the others waiting."

"You'll excuse me, won't you, Susanna? A group of us are going out to lunch, and then we're of to Bressingham to see John Bloom's steam engines. I'll see you at Ravenscourt tomorrow."

Susanna's heart was heavy as she saw Mandy take Mark's arm and smile up at him. It was obvious for all to see how things were between those two.

When Timothy Carstairs came for his piano lesson on Monday he said confidentially, "James Davidson tells me you're a famous concert pianist, and I wanted to know if it was true."

"In a way, yes—at least I was a few years back, at any rate." Susanna explained to him as best she could and the boy nodded seriously.

"Yes, I knew there was something special about you when I heard you playing at your cottage. When I'm famous I shall say that it was all because of you. Will you tell me all about the concerts you've performed in some time?" Susanna promised that she would.

The rest of the week passed without further incident. Susanna felt considerably happier about the rehearsals for the Speech Day presentation. Friday came at last and she set out for London. When she arrived at Liverpool Street station Ivor Kavanagh, the orchestra's present pianist, was waiting at the barrier. He caught her in a bear hug.

"Susanna, I just can't believe you're actually here after all this time. We've all missed you fearfully," he told her.

"It's wonderful to see you again too, Ivor," she said, and was filled with mounting excitement at the prospect of what lay ahead.

When she walked into the concert hall, Susanna was overwhelmed by greetings until at last Ralph said caustically: "All this is very touching, but we came here to rehearse. You will have plenty of time to speak with Miss Rosenfield later on— and now to work!"

By the end of that rehearsal Susanna felt both physically and emotionally drained. She had given it her all and still Ralph was not satisfied. She felt more relaxed after visiting the hairdressing salon where they had managed to fit her in for a trim and blow wave. Later she phoned her sister to make sure that her father had arrived safely and then, glancing into the hotel bar, she saw Ralph moodily contemplating his whisky, his forehead furrowed in a deep frown. She went to join him and he pulled out a chair for her.

"Hallo sweetheart, did you phone your sister?"

"Yes, my father's arrived and they're both looking forward to the concert tomorrow. What's wrong, Ralph? You look as if you've got all the troubles of the world on your shoulders."

He smiled wryly. "I'm just having a spot of trouble with my lead violinist Christabel Vernon, that's all. She was a bit temperamental this afternoon, as you no doubt noticed." He did not enlarge, merely added, "Oh Susie, and I do so want this concert to be a success."

"And I'm sure it will be, Ralph," she assured him more confidently than she felt and then, trying to sound casual, she asked, "Wasn't Christabel Vernon the girl you were having an affair with prior to your divorce?"

He looked startled and then spread his hands expressively. "Yes, but that's all over now, I assure you. I've found you again, my darling, so whyever should I need anyone else?" But Susanna was suddenly not convinced that he was telling her the truth. Later she sought out Ivor Kavanagh. She located him in the lounge reading a newspaper.

"Ivor, you've got to tell me the truth. Just what is this problem between Ralph and Christabel Vernon?"

Ivor sighed. "I'm afraid it's a bit delicate, Susie."

She smiled. "I'm fully aware that they had an affair—if that's what you mean."

He looked relieved. "They split up just before Ralph got his divorce and, since then, relationships between them have been decidedly strained. A few weeks back Christabel threatened to leave the orchestra. Then, in Paris, she and Ralph had a real humdinger of a row. That was after he'd been over here to see you. She's being extremely uncooperative at present because she wanted to play a violin concerto in tomorrow's concert and Ralph insisted that he wanted you to play the Rachmaninov. If you want my honest opinion then I reckon she's still crazy about Ralph, and that she's insanely jealous of you."

"Let's get this straight, Ivor, are you trying to tell me that Ralph came to find me on the rebound after his affair with Christabel had finished?" she demanded, suddenly feeling rather sick inside.

Ivor looked awkward. "Oh no, it wasn't exactly like that, Susie. I think he genuinely wanted to find you to make amends for the way he had treated you. You see, things have never been quite the same somehow since you left. Ralph was devastated when you went off—as we all were. On several occasions since then he has seen the orchestra on the verge of falling apart. Only Christabel has held it together. She's a brilliant violinist and, in spite of her temperament, an excellent leader. He's terrified that if she leaves, the orchestra will go downhill. Ralph sees you as a kind of good-luck charm, Susie.

He's often said that he was sure that if only he could find you again then things would be all right."

"But his concerts in England have been excellent," she argued.

"Yes, it's true that he hasn't lost his touch, but he upsets people and then there are problems. His bad humour has lost him several talented players, and even cost him a couple of concerts. If the orchestra keeps changing then one just doesn't get it in harmony—if you follow me. You are outstanding and he believes that you can put the orchestra back into the limelight again. People remember that you were Ralph's protégée—that you made your debut under him. Ralph thinks that the very act of giving you a comeback will raise him in the estimation of the public."

"In other words, Ralph is just using me in order to gain publicity for the orchestra!" she gasped.

Ivor looked uncomfortable. "I wouldn't put it quite so strongly as that, Susie, although I'll admit that if you were to rejoin the orchestra on a permanent basis he would probably regard you as a kind of insurance policy in case Christabel decided to leave. Then he would be able to say, 'Well never mind, I've still got Susanna Rosenfield.' Having you would bring him prestige. We've got no-one else of your calibre or Christabel's in the orchestra at the present moment." He looked worried. "Susie, maybe I'm speaking out of turn, but I couldn't bear to see you hurt again. Believe you me, Ralph genuinely does care for you, always has done, but, in a strange sort of way, he needs Christabel Vernon too."

Susanna passed a hand wearily across her forehead remembering Ralph's drawn face, the half-empty whisky bottle. "I had absolutely no idea about all this, Ivor. I thought everything was going as well as ever. Thank you for explaining the situation to me. Look, can't you talk with Christabel, tell her she's got an equally important role to play tomorrow? I'm sorry if it appears that I've stolen her thunder—but it really wasn't my intention."

"I'll see what I can do," Ivor promised.

Susanna did not set eyes on Ralph again that evening. She supposed she ought to have felt depressed by what Ivor had told her, but instead she was oddly relieved, for he had unwittingly helped her to finally decide upon the answer that she must give Ralph to his proposal of marriage.

Much to everyone's relief, Christabel Vernon put in an appearance the following morning looking calm, composed and extremely attractive. Susanna never did discover just what Ivor Kavanagh had said to her. The rehearsals bucked up as the day progressed and everyone seemed to be more relaxed. Susanna had almost forgotten what hard work it was preparing for a concert. There was scarcely time to grab a sandwich at lunch.

When Susanna eventually returned to the hotel a porter handed her a florist's box containing a single orchid with the message: "Good luck for tonight, love Mark." Her heart glowed and she was suddenly spurred on to play as she had never played before. She pinned the orchid to the shoulder of her evening gown.

Ralph came to see her in the dressing-room before the concert was due to begin. "Susie, you look magnificent!" he told her.

Her gown, purchased in Leeds over half-term, was a shimmering sea-green disclosing her creamy throat and shoulders. The hotel's hairdresser had come to her room and arranged her hair, sweeping back the sides into a knot and leaving the rest to fall in a cascade of shining waves. For jewellery she wore the silver locket that had belonged to her mother and the diamond earrings. She felt positively radiant.

"Who gave you the orchid?" Ralph demanded.

"Just an admirer," she told him laughingly. He kissed her then.

"Susie, there's a whole army of press

photographers and camera men from the TV studio downstairs clamouring to see you—do you think you could bear to face them?"

She smiled knowing how much the publicity meant to him and taking a deep breath said, "Yes, of course—lead me to them."

The first half of the concert went well; Christabel Vernon played brilliantly and then after the interval it was time for Susanna's performance at last. Ralph announced her himself: "For the second half of our concert this evening, we are delighted to welcome back to our orchestra—Susanna Rosenfield."

Susanna moistened her lips and looked nervously down at her hands and then she was on the stage. She hardly heard the rest of Ralph's words as she moved across to the piano as if in a dream, and then her heart almost missed a beat for there, sitting two rows from the front with Judy, Catherine and her father, was Mark. He cared enough at least to be present, and suddenly she knew that everything would

314

be all right because she would be playing for him. She acknowledged the tremendous applause that went up from the audience and then took her seat at the Steinway.

She played her own compositions first in which she had tried to capture the mood of the Norfolk countryside, the forestry, the glorious skies, the wild beauty of it all and lastly the sea—Blakeney Quay and the day at Brancaster. She received a resounding applause as she concluded and then came the biggest test of her life—the Rachmaninov.

Ralph smiled at her encouragingly and then his baton came down and she began to play. As her fingers flew over the keys she could feel a prickle of perspiration on her forehead, but by the time she was halfway through the first movement she knew that she was playing as never before. It was as if her whole soul came into the music, her heart, her very being, everything she possessed.

At last it was over and her heart sang for she knew that she had excelled herself.

Ralph led her amongst the most tumultuous applause out onto the front of the stage where she curtsied. The encores persisted until she was obliged to play part of the Allegro again. She was given a reception such as she had never before experienced even on the European tours. She was presented with a bouquet of apricot roses, and flowers were tossed onto the stage from every direction. She stood there her heart soaring—only having eyes for Mark who was smiling at her.

"I think we had all forgotten the magic Susanna Rosenfield possesses in those fingers of hers," Ralph said at last. "We will finish this evening's concert, ladies and gentlemen, with a tribute to her—for you then, Susanna, my own composition *Susanna's Song.*" And Ivor Kavanagh seated himself at the piano.

Afterwards cheers filled the hall. When they had died away Ralph bowed again and then, catching Susanna and Christabel Vernon each by a hand, pulled them back onto the stage so that they could both share the accolades together.

Later there was to be a party back at the hotel in Susanna's honour, but first she spoke with her guests. Judy was enraptured.

"Susie, that was quite the most beautiful thing I have ever heard, and just wait until Annabel sees that dress!"

Catherine congratulated her warmly; her father hugged her affectionately.

"Susie, you have surpassed yourself tonight. It was an outstanding performance and I'm very proud of you, darling."

Mark stood there silently watching on and then he added quietly, "It was a brilliant performance, Susie, better even than in Vienna. You are to be congratulated," and her heart sang. They all declined to stay on for the party except for Mark. Robert Price offered to drive Judy to Mark's friends where she was spending the night.

At last Susanna found herself alone with Mark.

"Are you really sure you want me to stay?" he asked her softly.

"Oh, yes, I do," she breathed. "Could you just wait here for me a few moments? I have to find Ralph. There's something important I must tell him."

Ralph was standing on the platform of the now empty auditorium as if reliving the concert all over again. He smiled as she came to his side.

"Susie, you were absolutely marvellous. I have truly never heard you play better. Thank you, my darling. Do you feel that you are ready to resume your career now?"

Susanna swallowed hard, knowing that what she had to say required courage. "I've enjoyed this concert tonight more than I had believed possible, Ralph, but for me it's been a kind of grand finale. Yes, I will play at the Aldeburgh Music Festival—if they ask me—or in any local concerts, but as for any more tours . . ." She shook her head. "That part of my life is over for ever, Ralph." She paused slightly. "A week ago you asked me to marry you and I promised to give you my answer tonight. Whilst I shall always regard you as a very dear friend who has taught me a great deal and inspired me to play in the way that I did tonight, I'm afraid that my answer must be no, because you see, Ralph, I don't love you any more—but thank you for asking me." She had decided not to mention Christabel.

Ralph took her hand between his. "When I saw you speaking with Mark Liston just now, then I think I knew your answer, Susie. He's won your heart, hasn't he?"

She nodded, suddenly filled with emotion, and reaching up kissed him gently on the cheek. "Thank you for asking me to play tonight. I'll remember this concert for the rest of my life." She took the engagement ring from her evening purse and handed it to him, but he did not take it.

"Keep it as a memento of the happy times we've spent together, Susie, and as a thank-you for the way in which you have boosted the morale of both my orchestra and myself tonight."

Mark was waiting for Susanna in the entrance hall. He steered her through the remaining throng of reporters and members of the public—who were still hovering outside the hall hoping to catch a last glimpse of her—to his waiting car. He drove her down into a narrow back street and parked. It was a mild June evening. There were stars in a sky of cobalt blue. She told him briefly what had passed between her and Ralph.

"For the past few weeks I've been living in cloud-cuckoo-land, but this life isn't for me—I realise that now. I have proved to myself what I am capable of and I've achieved more than I had dared hope for, but now I'm content to settle down in Bridgethorpe and to continue my piano teaching. I'm just glad that I've come to my senses in time, before I made a dreadful mistake. Thank you for coming tonight, Mark."

"Susie, there's something I must say. Judy told me how miserable you were on your birthday. She wasn't betraying a confidence, just trying to help. I was just so incredibly jealous that I'm afraid I misconstrued the situation."

"I thought you were no longer interested in me," she said, her heart thumping wildly.

"Oh, my darling, how wrong you were. I just wanted you to be happy. Shall we walk by the river for a bit?" She nodded and he took her arm. "When I met you in Vienna, I was fiercely attracted to you. I couldn't get you out of my mind then. It is almost as if we were destined to meet again. My attraction soon turned to love, but I knew that you still carried a torch for Ralph and that one day he would come back to claim you, and so I could not bring myself to tell you how I felt. I tried hard to get you out of my mind; it was hell seeing you at Ravenscourt every day and knowing you could never be mine and then, when Ralph turned up, I knew that any hope I might have had was gone. Mandy was there wanting escorts, demanding a good time, and so I started showing an interest in her, but all the time it was you I thought about."

"You even brought her here to London over half-term," she said quietly.

He laughed. "We stayed with the same friends of my parents that Judy and myself are staying with tonight. It was all perfectly innocent."

"Oh, Mark, if only we had been open with one another. Ralph swept me off my feet temporarily. I'm fond of him, I always shall be, but I don't love him any more. You see Ralph and I are soulmates, on the same plane where music is concerned. He spurred me on to fulfil my greatest ambition—to make that recording of the Rachmaninov concerto. He made me attain great heights, and drove me to perform in the way that I did tonight. But now there is no need for me to prove anything to myself any more, for I have discovered my true vocation in teaching."

The lights reflected in the river. Mark caught her in his arms.

"Oh, Susie, I do love you."

"You've never said that before," she breathed.

"I didn't dare say it—I couldn't bear the thought of being spurned."

He kissed her tenderly. "Oh, my dear love, it was a terrible time when I thought I had lost you for ever. If it hadn't been for Judy I should never have known the truth."

"Dear Judy . . . Oh, Mark, you've made me so very happy. You helped me to play the way I did tonight too. I played from my very heart."

"I know, my darling, and you reached right out to mine." His lips sought her and he swept her away into a magical enchanted world. Her heart sang for he loved her.

There were some marvellous reviews in the morning's papers. One of them read:

Susanna Rosenfield has stolen the hearts of millions making a rare appearance at a London charity concert which was broadcast last night. She brought enchantment to the evening playing the

323

romantic second Rachmaninov piano concerto. She is surely one of the most outstanding pianists of our time.

Miss Rosenfield has apparently been living in Norfolk during the past two years where she teaches music at Ravenscourt College, Bridgethorpe.

The news circulated amongst the villagers of Bridgethorpe and Susanna was welcomed home as some kind of heroine. Everyone looked at her with new eyes and Mrs. Gotobed proudly informed all and sundry that her next-door neighbour was ever such a famous pianist who had played on the radio.

Mark and Susanna now worked with renewed vigour at the *Daniel Jazz* with the result that the musical presentation on Speech Day was a resounding success. It was Timothy Carstairs who stole the show however with his rendering of *Jesu Joy of Man's Desiring*. Susanna felt a warm glow of pride inside her as she sat listening to him and realised that she was gaining as much pleasure because he was one of her pupils, as if she had been playing the music herself.

Ralph had given his word that he would keep his promise to Tim and help him with his career. Susanna knew that she would always be grateful to him for that. The London concert had had such good reviews that Ralph's confidence in himself had been restored; in fact, everything had turned out remarkably well.

"Congratulations, Miss Price," Graham Bryant said. "You and Mr. Liston between you have done an excellent job —even George Purbright was impressed with the standard of the performance!"

The Head wandered away to talk with some parents and Timothy Carstairs promptly appeared by her elbow.

"I've brought you some tea, Miss Price. It's so crowded in the common room that I thought perhaps we could sit outside."

"Why, thank you, Tim. What a good idea."

As they settled themselves on the seat under the arching branches of the enormous cedar tree on the lawn he said: "Mr.

Purbright agrees that I would be better to continue to have my lessons with you until I leave Ravenscourt. He says he doesn't mind because he started me on my way—jolly decent of him, wasn't it?"

"Yes," she agreed, amused. "Have you heard what you're doing in the summer yet?"

His face lit up. "Yes, I had a letter from my father yesterday, as a matter of fact. He's coming to England on leave in August, after all, and he's promised to take James Davidson and myself on a camping holiday to Scotland."

"Well, that is good news. He'll be able to fix up with Mr. Ewart-James about your music then too."

The boy nodded. "Thanks, Miss Price, for all you've done this term to help me."

She smiled. "That's all right, Tim. I'm only glad things have worked out so well for you."

There was a faraway look in his eyes as he said, "One day I'll compose a piece of music for you too—you'll see!" And she was sure that he would, for Timothy

Carstairs had the sort of determination that it took to get to the top.

After the parents had gone it suddenly seemed remarkably quiet and Susanna was aware of an anti-climax. Mark sought her out and they walked beyond the school and across the fields. It was a beautiful summer's evening; the sky was an expanse of metallic blue streaked with pink from the setting sun. In the distance a skylark winged its way home. Mark slipped an arm about her waist.

"Well, it's over and Tim Carstairs played from the very heart too."

She smiled up at him. "Yes, I know, bless him. He'll go a long way, that boy."

"And it will be all thanks to you." He caught her in his arms. "Oh, Susie, I do so love you. Are you ready to accept me into your heart? I want you to share my life with me—to be my wife, so will you marry me, my darling?"

She met his amber-flecked brown eyes with her own shining midnight-blue ones. "Oh yes, Mark, I'll marry you," she breathed softly.

He kissed her then and her heart was filled with the music of love. It was surely the most beautiful concerto of all.

THE END

Other titles in the
Linford Romance Library:

A YOUNG MAN'S FANCY
by Nancy Bell

Six people get together for reasons of their own, and the result is one of misunderstanding, suspicion and mounting tension.

THE WISDOM OF LOVE
by Janey Blair

Barbie meets Louis and receives flattering proposals, but her reawakened affection for Jonah develops into an overwhelming passion.

MIRAGE IN THE MOONLIGHT
by Mandy Brown

En route to an island to be secretary to a multi-millionaire, Heather's stubborn loyalty to her former flatmate plunges her into a grim hazard.

SHADOW DANCE
by Margaret Way

When Carl Danning sent her to interview the elusive Richard Kauffman, Alix was far from pleased—but the assignment led her to help Richard repair the situation between him and his ex-wife. If only she could sort out the situation between herself and Carl!

WHITE HIBISCUS
by Rosemary Pollock

"A boring English model with dubious morals," was how Count Paul Santana Demajo described Emma. But what about the Count's morals, and who is Marianne?

STARS THROUGH THE MIST
by Betty Neels

Secretly in love with Gerard van Doorninck, Deborah should have been thrilled when he asked her to marry him. However, he had made it clear that he wanted a wife for practical not romantic reasons.